The Uncertain

Written by: Gustavo Lomas
Edited by: Sierra Rhodes

This book is for you. Your life has influenced the life of this book and for that I thank you.

Questions

For as long as I can remember I had been questioning the world around me, questioning its meaning and inquiring for it to include me so that I would no longer feel disconnected. I had always been looking for answers without knowing what questions deserved my attention, wondering aimlessly, in search of a cure for my curiousity. It had always been my wondering that pushed me to wander from place to place, which is what brought me to be where I was.

I was in a room, in a room that was part of what used to be someone's home, but to me it was just some place full of unknowns with left over nothings from people who had been there before me. Yet all I wished to do was question the world I could barely make out through the window; I had a whole place to myself and what lay beyond the room where I stood is where my attention lay. I stared out at the world, the one I had learned to live in, but at the same time always felt lost in, and searched for clarity through a grubby window.

I can think best to describe what had happened as a world wide refinement. Not one caused by antagonists or governments but those and other aspects like it did play a part. What happened is the result of humanity coming to a decision as a whole, as we made the choice to reshape our world and lives in order to truly better our future. I guess the old phrase for the idea was "exactness," but that was always simply an idea that guided us to a reality we produced; yet I felt the world remained to be at odds with us, its inhabitants. There were no longer any boundaries or labels, just people of all types who lived simply to enjoy yet, I had so many questions.

"Where will I be in the future when I look back at this moment? What if at this moment, I am looking back on my past, remembering myself asking this question?"

That had always been my favorite question to ask myself as a child. It allowed me to remember how much bigger the world was compared to me while at the same time, it offered me some insight into my mind. I remembered the seemingly blank look I would get on my face as I asked it, how it would occur to me at the most inopportune times and trail me through my inner conscious. Even as I stood in that unused space it made me wonder, it made me question where I was, where I had been and where I might be going.

I stood alone, just me and the abandoned furniture that sat in stillness and gathered dust from the air. The air itself felt neglected, it felt as though it did not want to be a part of the room, it did not want to be inhaled because it felt polluted by the past it had been forced to be part of and the future it could not deny.

The air was there long before the furniture therefore, it had been a part of the vast history of the room. It remembered the first time it had its first companions, the frustration of the people who lived there and the desperation they let intermingle into the air. In the air

3

there were stories of loss, of hope, of pain and of compassion but the air also had its own story it wished to be known. It had a story of longing and disappointment and as I breathed, I saw these things and I felt them, each memory, each dream, and each good-bye. It seemed the air was ashamed to allow me to know such things, just as I felt ashamed to share my regrets with it with each breath I took, as it unwillingly had allowed me into its memories. It had been so long since it had someone to connect with that beneath its discomfort, there were hints of subconcious appreciation.

I felt an odd sense of welcome. Odd because this was not a place I had been in before, but I felt as though I were already familiar to the atmosphere. I began to accept the surroundings as they were, dusty and stale but open to strangers. I ran my hands across the furniture as I walked by, as if to get to know it better. The couch sat still by a wall and was covered in a sheet but it seemed as though it were playing its own game of "hide and seek". I smiled for I did not let it know I had found it just yet. The dining room table had two chairs tucked underneath it, the two of them waiting to be put to use during the next meal while the table itself eagerly awaited its chance at supporting the weight of said meal. The oven, stove and refrigerator all held on to the hope of being opened once more and fulfilling their purpose. There were a few cabinets in the kitchen as well that were old but not broken down. I gave them no second thought because I knew I wouldn't be there long. On my walk to get acquainted with this place, my life long ability to see, feel and recognize the lost history of the area had proven to be once again useful. The outside world's knowledge however, continued to escape my mental grasp.

Since I had already been welcomed by some of the inanimate objects that were left behind, I began to rearrange them in order to help me try to make sense of the world. I rested my jacket on the kitchen table in an effort to ease its longing and once again put its legs to use. I took one chair and set it in the center of the middle room and as I did I felt the other develop some jealously for having been left behind. I slowly approached the couch and pulled the sheet off of it. A sense of surprise arose with the sheet in the air as it flapped and floated down. I used a corner of it to wipe the dust from the window before throwing it back over the couch. I could feel myself beginning to settle into my surroundings, beginning to lower my guard in an unfamiliar place.

I stood and faced the window before moving the chair around the room, until I felt it was somewhere that would benefit my purpose. I moved it from the center of the room to the side, to the next room near the couch and then back to the original room just in front of the window. It made sense for me to set it there and so it sat for a few seconds before I turned it around so that it faced the inside of the room. With my back towards the window as I leaned against the window pane, I stared at the chair with concern as though I were sure it could not bear the burden I would soon put on it.

Now you, like me, face vague opportunities that have been wielded by indefinite knowledge...

As this sentence unraveled in my mind, I began to feel the chair probing my actions, attempting to make sense of what was happening. I decided as I should say something to ease the uncertainty that lingered in the air.

"I must apologize to you. I must ask for your forgiveness... I have made you my sacrifice, just as others have made me theirs."

I hesitated briefly as if waiting for an acknowledgement of my apology. The chair did nothing to recognize my efforts. Oddly however, I was content with having no reaction, it was what I had come to expect. The silence between the two of us, although brief, further invoked my muted remorse.

"Your current state of being should be blamed on the lack of being in others, those who you will not know and who refuse to know you. But I have learned you cannot be upset with others for the faults they have placed on you."

Nothing more was said to my unwilling companion; the two of us sat in our silence waiting regretfully for answers. It was in this landscape of empathy, this scene of loss that I was met by confusion.

I turned away and took a few steps back from the window, putting distance between myself and my accidental hostage. As I stood in the stillness of the room, I could not ignore my mind's prying nature. Concepts about the world began to flow into my psyche, tormenting me in the isolation. Struggling against the crushing weight of psychological seclusion, I spoke the thoughts I was able to grasp out loud.

"Questions prime curiosity for the unknowns it will one day dream of..."

I paused but answers continued to escape my comprehension. I began to realize that questions had come to be all I was able to understand; I was anxious to find some way to delay intellectual chaos. I felt the pressure of the room, the desire of my new acquaintances who wanted me to share what I was feeling with them. Now the room that suggested sanctuary seemed to be clustered with nothing; the only hint of recognition was sunlight that invaded the room through the window. I stood and stared at the window for a moment before turning the chair around so that I could rest on it if the world's confusion became too heavy for me to stand.

"...in those dreams it will realize all the truths that have stemmed from fiction, this will in turn help it to see many fictions that have been declared as truths..."

I turned and stood face to face with the window, my faded reflection staring back at me, insisting I wait but pushing me to sit down, to look out and attempt to make sense of the insane world put before me; the insane world that had easily named me as the lunatic.

Gazing out at an opaque horizon I found myself further lost in abandonment. I sat at a window looking out at the sunset, yet I felt I was the one being observed.

"...Although the world may be fictitious, it is based on many truths." I said towards my wilted likeness, "Truths that can be denied by many facts... and facts conceived during misfortune in life..."

I looked down at the floor feeling ashamed and damaged, wondering if I in fact was the insanity that plagues the world; I tried to console myself. *I have made sense of the unspoken doubts, individually analyzed all of the certainties and realized that insanity is its own oxymoron...*

That was my way of trying to scold the world for naming me so poorly. As I stared past the horizon, continuing to feel no sense of difference in my vision I spoke again to my faded image.

"The world had always held within it potential for salvation, hope and a future. Yet within countless minds were misfortunes, millions of seconds of heartache, and the misshapen views of a tattered and lonely soul."

Surprised by the ease at how certain I was with what I said and saddened by the reality of it, I asked myself... *What is left when a world's soul is no longer recognizable..?*

"The human spirit has been abandoned and left alone to wallow in angst at what it does not know..."

That spirit had become irrelevant because it was made to sit alone in silence, much like I do now, to contemplate itself in an attempt to clarify the present as an unrestricted place...

Relentless thoughts of mourning and turmoil began to pile up and race through my mind yearning to be recognized and released, with only the desire of being let go as their motive. I allowed each and

7

every idea its wish letting them all stream freely from my head while still allowing others to only reveal themselves in my mind.

"Simple freedoms were regarded as pointless because they had only been understood for their prospective future."

The world was inhabited by prisoners who were all plagued by curiosity's correlation to what and why, but wanted nothing more than to simply be.

...What is a logical question; but it is not the one that we should be asking. The true question of importance is why. Why? Because it is simple, however, it does not allow its answers that same luxury.

I paused briefly before letting the thought continue.

A word comprised of three letters, three letters that contain so much mystery. Wherever there is life, why is the question that is most asked yet at the same time the question whose answers continue to elude us. What is not the question we wish to be answered, because then all we would have obtained is the action and not the reason or depth behind it...

In the window my dim reflection stared back at me and appeared to be passing judgment of my actions and thoughts. I stood and watched it for a moment questioning its reasoning before backing away and allowing it to fade, as I wondered why. I stepped back so that I could be in the center of the room and try to answer my own questions.

"In time," I said aloud, hoping to ease the pressure of the burdening awareness of my mind. "In time nothing is left to be only a mistake. The reason there is reason is to understand the misunderstood."

I waited and pondered this statement for a moment trying to shed light on the truth that lay beneath it.

8

"So much was misunderstood. So much was without reason. Even worse is the fact that illogical reasoning had become the basis of existing. In our dreams rests our deprived hope, hope to acquire all we have lived without, all we blindly desire. Ideas of reality have been written down in the past for us to learn about in the future, ideas built on a foundation free of disbelief. Ideas founded around logical interpretations of pure human wishes, simplicities endowed onto us naturally... love, compassion, truth and innocence."

I stopped for a moment and shook my head in an effort to unravel a few answers, rubbing my neck as I continued to think.

Innocence once meant purity, once meant good. Then it became known as a fading memory, a soon to be lost legacy. That is part of the story told us, the future generations, in hopes of restoring its once prominent definition. Things-everything-that had once been associated with innocence for a long time stopped being seen as such. We now read about such signs like, single roses once given as a sign of love, devotion and passion. How a sunrise was once viewed as simple innocence. Many of us have read about such things and have been inspired by them once again, but those before us could rarely be engulfed by the feeling of true innocence.

For too long a flower was a sign of misfortune, of death, so they were only given to those you felt remorseful for. The sun, whether it rises or sets, reminds us of a world we were left with, a world created upon despair which makes it hard to forget the destruction and grief that is slowly fading away behind the beauty. We grew up being taught about the illusion of peace in hopes of carrying on the importance of stopping the illusion and making it into a reality. As peace, for far too long, could not have been thought of as an illusion, it was always only a mirage, something people thought was there because they wanted it to be.

I began pacing back and forth through the three rooms rubbing my eyes and head, as thoughts relentlessly raced into my mind, too fast to for me to sort through silently.

"...Logical truth, the logic behind humanity's forgotten truths, has diminished over time..."

I did not know why this thought was the one I spoke out of the jumble of them in my head but I hoped it would help me gain a deeper understanding of the uncompromising presence of a forgotten hope. Then I looked down momentarily and saw a book I did not realize was sharing the space with me. This somehow allowed me to redirect my mental focus.

Just outside of the doorway between the center room and bedroom it sat on the floor. Even then I had to question.

"How long have you been observing me?"

I felt it would have shrugged if it had shoulders, but as I approached it I was hesitant in reaching out my hand to pick it up, cautious of whether or not it should be touched. Fearful of myself not being ready, I stood over it for a minute then backed away slightly before turning around to continue pacing, going from one room to another but focusing on the book as if it were the answer.

*   *   *

The book seemed to follow me like a painting I had seen on a wall once. It was at an abandoned museum I had stumbled upon while traveling. In the painting there was a lady with two kids sitting on her lap in a garden and for some reason the eyes of the kids were painted on at just the right angle to where they seemed to follow me, it made me nervous and uncomfortable and I left soon after. With every step I took that is what I felt from the book, like it was following me, demanding more of my focus and distracting me from trying to gather my thoughts. Out of frustration only and without really thinking, I walked straight towards it and picked it up. Then tossed it onto the table and let it lay there, I guess to regain what little control I had had. I couldn't decide if I wanted to leave it behind or include it as part of my belongings.

After a few minutes. I grew impatient with myself and momentarily thought of giving the book credit for its patience. I tucked it into my inner jacket pocket before putting my jacket on and then gathered all I had and stood once more in the middle room. I looked around as if accepting the farewell, the appreciation and respect between that place and myself. Some how able to understand the detachment I would feel once I was gone. Before reaching for the door I took one more look at the empty chair and felt a sense of sorrow come over me, along with an adopted trust.

Outside it was bright but it was a luminance that was far from natural and all too familiar. The streets were empty but not without sound. I looked around still trying to make sense of what I saw. I began to step in a direction before stopping myself and walking the opposite way. It felt as though I had walked in both directions before but the one I chose gave me hope in clarifying all that remained unclear. There were familiar landmarks and unfamiliar signs on a path I had gone down before, and even voices in the distance as I wandered on, and my mind continued to be filled with questions and thoughts of things that nobody had ever seemed to understand.

"Logical truth…" I said again. still no idea as to what it is. "… Prompted by illogical time…"

With no true destination in mind and a new annoyance in the shape of a book in my pocket. a book I feared, yet anticipated would create more questions, I continued to wander.

I suddenly found myself in a small house. and inside there was the empty air I accepted as company. and it greeted me in the same manner it always had. I grin at the sight of an empty open fire place. and shrugged off the attempted welcoming of stairs.

Full paged empty books sat on a shelf, with titles that had always seemed tedious and uninventive. I searched for a spot to become comfortable, different from the one I had the night before simply because I could not remember where I had been. and began to

11

analyze the book I had blindly carried. After taking it out of my jacket and looking it over, I saw there was no author and no description anywhere of what resided beneath the surface. Only two words on the cover, I assumed they were the title, Empty Filling. Two words and not so much as a hint of their description. Before even opening the book I had began to question its meaning, striving to prematurely evaluate its contents, and more so foresee an ending. I glanced up in an effort to distract my curious mind, only to have another book catch my attention. *Why have I never noticed that book before?*

The title horizontally upside down, read: A Life of Religion. The last word seemed almost foreign to me although I knew I had seen it before.

"Religion..." I said to myself in an effort to weed out the definition from my psyche. Drawing a blank and too curious to attempt to remember why I had forgotten the second book, I got up from my seat to look at it, nevertheless noticing this book too had no author, although there was a small paragraph on the back cover, it read:

"In a world full of opinions, I have found that faith is the source from which we derive each and every one of them. Behind each system of faith instilled in us, there are ideals that we dispense within ourselves based on feeling. As people, as human beings, we easily accept and hold onto hope. Occasionally hope seems to come from no where, and at times it is carried with us in order to obtain overall betterment. But when did we gather the idea of hope? Why does it hold such value to us when any person can obtain it? Where does it come from? Throughout the duration of my life, I sought out the origin of hope, only to find the answer in the palm of my hands."

As I sat in the dark looking out through a window, one completely different from the first, I realized my eyes set a goal for themselves. They wished to see nothing happen. I had been staring just to know for a single moment there was nothing out there.

Waiting for the view to take away from my thoughts, and allow me to admit to accepting uncertainty in order to rest.

I looked back at the two books that had found me hours before and glared at them both with a look of desperation. I blamed them for my unfulfilled curiosity. even though I knew my curiosity was displeased long before seeing them. The two books sat with me in silence. mocking my inquisitive agony with their calm, yet shrill, unread knowledge. Behind the two books the fireplace crackled; although I did not remember lighting it I did not question how it had come to life nor did I question why I had not questioned it until that moment. It spewed out small wisps of smoke that had slowly begun to fill the room and I sat there dully. allowing each small cloud to darken the space around me.

The window gradually became indistinguishable; as the ridiculing hush of the two books grew more evident. Even through the smoke I could feel their presence almost as if they fed on the fire. If I had wanted to walk I would have had no room, and although I apparently knew the room I had no vision of my surroundings. This realization would not have bothered me otherwise but at this moment my brain could not stand anymore unknowns. As I sat alone wanting nothing more than to know a voice spoke out.

"Open the window…"

"Excuse me?" I asked, almost surprised at how calmly I answered, I felt almost relieved to hear a sound in the dark. No response. I waited a few seconds before speaking out in no particular direction. "What do you mean? I… I can't find the window anymore…"

A whisper from behind me. "Open the window…"

In my life it had always been easy for me to commit to many things I had not been sure of. many things that others could not oblige to out of fear. Now I found myself unable to completely commit to something I myself grew afraid of. turning to see the face beneath the voice. I found myself in the place where others had long been before me, somewhere I had never before been able to understand. Because I could not fathom the feeling of being as others had been, the feeling of loss and disarray, I felt questions I did not want to ask building up inside me. I felt them at the tip of my mind, trying to drill themselves into my throat so they could escape and let themselves be known, despite my uncertainty and unwillingness. Out of foolishness I pleaded with myself to keep them in my psyche and allow them to unravel there and only there. I knew this would not ease my desperation but thinking seemed better than hearing them stated in my apprehensive voice.

How am I to make sense of such a feeling? How can I expect to know if I can not trust myself? What do I not trust myself to do? What am I failing to comprehend...? For as long as I can remember I have always dissuaded myself to be anywhere that involved knowing two sides of one occurrence. I have always gone in and triumphed when there was good but collapsed once there was bad. So, for the sake of never being wrong or let down, I have kept a distance between myself and what I have been part of. Even now that I have announced this fault to myself, I still hesitate to turn around. Not out of fear or misunderstanding, but because I can see the negative forming behind me. I can feel the unknown conjugating in an attempt to have me further torment myself about looking behind me. The voice has stopped; it is no longer beckoning for my attention-perhaps because it can observe the uncertainty in my mind? What ever the case, it is no longer here, there is only me...

The realization that I had decided to commit to not committing further disturbed me. I had made a choice to ignore the questionable simply because I did not want more uncertainty, becoming a hypocrite along side what I have so long been questioning. So for what seemed like a plaguing, pointless eternity I sat still, observing the unclear room and attempting to convince myself that nothing unfamiliar lay behind me.

I sat there and tried to think of nothing. I sat there and pleaded for my curiosity to control itself. In my mind I could only think of one thing, only one request to get the questions out of my head.

Leave me alone... I did not ask I made it a fact. I wanted to be left alone because then, I felt, the questions would be illogical. I kept repeating it in my mind.

Questions are illogical... Leave me alone... To me it seemed almost poetic and I could not help but be proud of some form of success and laugh at how it came when I felt I was failing.

Insanity

Mine was not the only laugh I heard. I was not sure if it was purely in my head or if it was in fact some sort of unforeseen companion in the room, nevertheless I knew it was something strange.

"Strange," I said to myself, or what I would hope was only myself.

All I have are inquiries. They are all I have yet I know they are non-loyal partners. Committed to me because my sanity is indistinguishable...committed to me because I am lost, so lost that I laugh when I know I should be afraid. I lay awake because all dreams seem to be nightmares and now, so it seems, is my reality. Why do I feel what I feel? Am I even feeling at all or is it simply...my desire to feel something, anything that drives me? All days seem to blend into times, while I seem to blend into nothing...

As yet another day ended, darkness began to gather all around me. Stationed in hesitation, I noticed the sunlight beginning to diminish. Allowing disorder to transform into me. No attempts to understand the disturbing negligence. No concept of time that had past, I had chosen unwillingly to lose it, to lose me, to lose my sanity. If I did in fact have any of it to begin with.

It is a strange thing to realize the slow dissolving of one's mental character but it is stranger still for that person to just watch from a distance as its happens. To give up without knowing what it is they sacrifice or to whom or where it is being sacrificed.

It's just me. Sitting in fear, paralyzed by disbelief; monitoring the little bit of sanity I am still able to maintain, rationing sanity throughout my skull, like a child would ration candy, desperate yet exceedingly weary.

My eyes glazed, seeing and observing without my knowledge; staring off with no true purpose yet still trying to decipher everything they see. My empty mind overflowing with decay, combined with repeating thoughts of misery, and repeating thoughts of nothing.

A societal ruin...fallen cities and empires...unable to avoid imminent collapse...destruction is human nature...

I no longer had questions, but felt I instead had all the answers. After all, I had plenty of nothing to reach for, plenty of nobody to understand; and as solitude began to creep through the room, I was well aware of the isolation that would be my time here.

I am all that resided in the center of doubt, accompanied by unpredictable questions that began to negate answers; and the simplest of answers began to lose all sense of transparency. Here I sat resting on insanity as the mocking still of night settled in.

In sanity, nothing is out of reach...

"Insanity however, puts reach into emptiness."

My mind began going, fading away allowing distress to be revived, I found myself lost in familiar unfamiliarity, knowing only suspicion of what I had known. Nothing, was now priceless and too far into my understanding. Depending on something so unconventional was a true test of my wit, but to test wit intentionally without panic or reason, was an act of abstract curiosity.

No voice of reason while attempting to deny the unknown. It seemed appropriate to acknowledge solidity under the circumstances. In my head...the nursing of my end began.

How do I describe such pain? A sense of longing that most see as pointless, if my eyes close, all that is becomes nothing that was. Insatiable grief, immense sorrow, timeless passion, unconditional devotion and fear that thrives if I close my eyes. Silence beckons for the return of my insanity. Heartbreak yields only to wait its turn. I blink, I'm lost, my tears no help, a sad mind, tempting insanity. Pain lives because its partners do not die. I cannot stand to try and close my eyes...

How I wished I could close my eyes. How I wanted nothing more than that small satisfying muscular movement, feeling as if it would nullify my lack of being.

Chaos was beginning to ride up my spine, slowly make its way into my unsteady self-awareness.

Was this the voice I heard beckon me to open the window? Suddenly panic arose *...it did not want to help me; it wanted to manipulate me into letting in the dysfunctional air and outside world. To make it easier to smother me in this smoke...if that is in fact what has clustered the room...*

Numb was I to what I was supposed to feel. The room was full of smoke but I did not feel myself gasping or coughing, I merely sat in it, to become a part of it or to be engulfed by it was unclear. A want to want to fight, a need to feel a need, but no hope to reach

19

out for any of these things. No hope of hope, only a sadistic point of view that I was fighting to comprehend as my own or someone else's.

Who would that someone else be? If I was seeing what they were meant to, then what was I suppose to be seeing? Was it that I was not seeing it because the other was no longer capable of sharing its view? Was I to be imprisoned in this...landscape...this...valley of despair?

"Answers are not what I am meant to acquire in this moment. In this time, in this unyielding tragic ambiance, all I am meant to hold is the slow glazed look that I am unsure of was not always there."

Circles, my mind kept going around in circles. Following the unfathomable, reaching for the unobtainable, chasing silence foolishly unaware it could not be caught for it was lost...

I am lost. Lost: unable to be found or discovered, a definition, pointless because I am, and feel, the indefinite unidentifiable inconvenience of intolerable isolation. Indifference, illogical, incomparable...words that begin with I but where does, did, do I begin?

No more smoke. No more room.

Has it been hours, minutes or days?

Nevertheless, I deemed the answer inappropriate, inapt for no matter where I might be or what once was or is, wasn't or isn't, I know I was not a part of it.

Circles...*where do I go from here*...circles...*how do I go from here*...

In circles...a loss of everything, or what should feel like everything. What should feel like, anything at all?

*Indirect, indiscretion, individual ideas, no, ideological instincts;
where is my mind, my mind did mind to be mine, it was mine but
what once was mine is no more, no more...there is no less but
there is no more...no more mind to what's mine.*

Only words, only words and my breath, my breathing but even
these things seemed out of control...

*Out of control, out of control, out of control...just words, out of
control. Breathe, breathing, out of control. Try, try to personify,
personalize, and prepare...pinpoint proper parallels. Why look for
parallels when it is a world of verticals crushed by hesitant
horizontals? Why look for lines when shapes are the difference?
Why look for anything at all, when everything seems to be
deniable? Deadly, disaster, distance, despair...just words to me,
just words, to me...to me they are me, I am them...all of them, they
are me. I am the lunatic, the world is sane, is tangible. No, I am
tangible, the world is sane...I am the lun-atic, lun-a-tic, lunatic...*

"All because I have the desire to no longer get lost."

I did not think of the books, I did not think of the forgotten
furniture. It was no help to me; I had no need for such sad and
desperate things, as I had become a sad and desperate thing.

*A thing...I cannot even recognize myself as a person or a being, I
have allowed myself to be known even in my thoughts as a "thing."
How? Why? What is it I had done wrong? What is it I had not
done? What is it, was it, could it be or was it to be anything at all?
All I want to do is be part of something, to feel change in such a
way that I would always be able to travel into that moment from
where ever I was in the future and know it was the time everything
changed. Not just for me but at the same exact time, for everything.
Is that too much to ask, to want?*

"In such a tragic place, developed from tragic times, how is it that
existing meant learning to neglect the very thing that made us
human? Or is that why we must only be human? Are we meant to

live in fear, in angst, because we do not deserve better and that is our great illusion? Do we believe in such a thing because we lack, and most times deny purposefully what it is we know we deserve and truly want?"

I had to try to calm myself...*this is not my world. I am doing the best I can with the beginning of the worst that could have been.*

Even still I could not help further question, further examine what it was. What the world was.

This is the truth yet because it was me who would announce it; they would deny it and still place me far out of their minds. I would be a plague to them. A mental illness, a logic seeking leper from which they should be saved. They would send me into a state of exile, so that they may live and be free, be blind...or am I blind? Is it me who is indulging in fantasies and inclinations because I want to be the outcast, the untouchable, the unknown undoing of previous generation's transgressions? Am I it? Am I the doing and un-doing of sanity's sanctuary, its rightful place in a world in which it seems unobtainable?

I felt I had begun to comprehend where it was I had been leading myself, a hint of development, be it coincidental or not, was appreciated in my consequential times.

This isn't me this isn't me at all. None of this feels right, none of this feels like this is where I am suppose to be.

If not here then where, how do I get there? Is it even a where I am suppose to get to or is it more likely a when?

Slowly my emptiness began to fill, I was unsure of with what or from where but I knew I grew tired of questions. I grew tired of reaching with the intent of never finding anything in my grasp when I pulled my hand back.

Could that be part of the problem? Putting much of the emphasis on what and where I am suppose to go instead of taking my time to get there. Can I really have time, do I have time, and does taking control mean letting go?

As much as I wanted to know what it was I seemed to be missing, I couldn't help but feel as though something about this place, something about me being there just didn't seem right.

This whole thing just doesn't seem, real...

*   *   *

Memoires

When I opened my eyes I could feel hints of panic still lingured. The back of my neck was cold with sweat and my hands were clenched in tight fists. As I sat there trying to make sense of what I had dreamt about, I couldn't help but feel as though I would not be getting much sleep. I wasn't sure if I wanted to really.

It was a dream...it was just a dream...but it seemed so real.

I don't remember falling asleep or sitting down again.

I got out of the chair to stretch and shake loose rements of my sleep. I looked out through the window and noticed that outside the sun had began to set, which made my decision to stay in the empty cluster of rooms much easier.

Since I had already been welcomed by the left over inhabitants of this place I began to really let myslelf settle in with my surroundings. The more I moved around the more I began to feel at ease, and then I recognized that I began to simply feel. I was unsure of what it meant but I did not want to ruin the reawakened sense of calm, my newfound sensation of simply being. I began to understand some forgotten pieces of my persona and purpose.

Would you all be willing to hear them? I thought in reguards to my adopted furniture. *Would you be willing to lend me your ears in order to help me make sense of the accidental progresses I may have made in my dream?*

"I remember..." I started to tell them, preparing to share with them an unknown story of my development. It seemed it was only right for me to share the bit of my past I had unlocked as they had so graciously opened up theirs to me.

"I remember a bit of my childhood. Bits and pieces really, both good and bad. But they are mine, and I hesitantly have come to claim them as such."

*I remember...*A smile formed in my lips. I did not remember the last time that had happened.

"I remember playing outside, trying my best to find anything new and exciting and maybe even get into a little bit of trouble. I was always driven by intrigue for you see, I had always been told that there was nothing left to find or do or say that had not been already. I never believed such lies, and so they only further fueled my conspicuous curiosity. I knew of wonder and thrill and excitement, long before I had learned of disappointment, fear and disbelief. I remember a place with trees, there was water, there was plenty of sun and shade but most importantly, there was my determination to be part of it all."

I felt each of my companions, my subjects as they seemed, listening closely, more intently. Anxious to find out more of what might happen but also equally excited to just feel a part of something once again, that was somehting we now had in common. They felt eased to have life near them and to have been given the reassurance that they were still able to serve a purpose to someone.

"There was a walkway near where I used to spend my days, and a small fence that was not well put together, you could tell by its appearance-it served as both a guide and prohibitory force for those too fearful of the unexplored. A small brown wooden fence, painted over to make it blend into its surroundings. I recall hopping over it to get started on my miniature quests, whether or not it was necessary I do not recollect but I know it added to the sense of wonder. I walked the path that I am sure has now been overtaken by plants."

Time's attempt to manipulate nature so that the paths of others could be forgotten no doubt, I thought.

"I looked down at the ground when I walked, to see if anything at my feet would lead to some sort of treasure or lost land. I always looked for things to climb or jump on or possibly both, mimicking what I would think an animal would do. My favorite walk way, one too small for any adult to tread through, went down towards the water, and as I walked down I always stopped and admired exactly what my eyes saw: the flowing trees, the wild berry bushes, the sounds of animals shuffling through the brush and the path that never seemed to forget how much I enjoy surprises. I also knew that what I didn't see would be far less kind but I appreciated and respected those aspects. Many different, and at the time, seemingly exotic plants were both in front of and behind me. I often wondered if they were trying to cover up my steps to make it more challenging for me to find my way back, but I welcomed the challenge; perhaps foolishly but eagerly. This place was always so beautiful, always so peaceful.

"Nothing beyond those moments was ever an issue and everything within them was all that mattered. Only when I was older did I notice that there was a road just on the other side; but still beyond the road was a hill, big enough to shelter a vast area from the sun but small enough to climb in the small part of a day. What I particularly remember about this hill however is, growing out of the side was a tree. It was not a big tree or one that bore fruit or was even significant to the vast hillside's demeanor. But I do remember it had flowers, only barely beginning to blossom when I saw them. I had always thought each flower, with each of its petals, was unique to one another, each one its own entity with their own purpose. Some would try to reach farther than the rest off the side of the hill, a few in an attempt to learn the story of how their tree came to be on such an odd place; most of them just wanted to absorb as much of the sun as possible in the day. Although quite possibly, there were those who wondered if they were as glorious and beautiful as the other flowers, not knowing it was still too soon to tell.

"Then there was the sky. It was clear and blue and it was above this silent ballet, but not too good for any of it-it was above because it had to be, because it had its own responsibility to fulfill. I felt it was often admiring the scenery with me once it received a break in pushing the clouds forward to where ever it was they were to be deployed. Most times I felt the sky was welcoming me from time to time to a reunion to which I had been overdue at arriving. I was unaware that my desire to be influenced was equal to that of the scenery's, which I had only thought of as a land of mystique, desire to be influential.

"After I had been back and forth a few times in what I had now come to know as the true world, it was almost instinctual knowing to mind where I stepped and rely on my surroundings. Rocks lead down to the water, to my then and still now, trained eyes they looked like they had been made to be stairs. It was only after time had passed, it seemed, the rocks had learned to pull themselves with much difficulty to new places they had wanted to reach or had quite possibly originally wanted to be. Despite my frustration at them for trying to confuse me, I used them regardless and not soon after found myself on my back in the sand. I remember my feet seemed to always move toward the water, I got excited any time I would look out at the boulders that I would dub my lily pads. My feet would begin to move and I was jumping and leaping from rock to rock, sometimes it felt as if the rocks were following me; cheering me on from beneath my feet, and they appeared when I needed them to, never allowing me to misstep or lose my focus. I was never sure of where I wanted to end up, whether it was just sitting on a boulder in the middle of the water or finding new paths to get me across and then back again. Once I began to let go and every movement and every thought became pure instinct, my next move would occur before I had time to think about the previous one."

A nature made game board. I admitted calling it to myself.

"I sometimes looked back after navigating over the water and smiled at the game I had played, proud to have tried something new and prouder still to have succeeded. The calm waterbed and I had agreed on rules. It would allow me some rocks or boulders and I would use them as best I could while attempting not to get wet. A slip of the foot here and there was all right, but once I fell in or got stuck with nowhere to go but backwards, I lost. But that rarely happened."

I stood up to give myself a break and to venture out into the other rooms in an attempt to find some way to keep myself warm during the night. The chair, I could feel, was growing tired of my weight, not because I was heavy but because it was out of practice. So out of understanding, I felt it was time for me to switch to something more comfortable. I moved it back under the table, pushed it in and patted it on the back. I saw no fireplace, which oddly relieved me after having woken up from my dream earlier. I instead decided I would rest on the couch. I found two candles on a dresser in the same room and hoped they would be enough to keep me warm, or at least held enough wick to help me get a make shift fire for myself.

What could I put the fire into? I did not want to burn my new sanctuary away. Squinting while I searched as the rooms began to grow darker: I was able to make out a small pail. *Metal, good, this will work.* I grabbed one of the candles, the smallest one. I realized I had nothing to light it with.

What are the odds? I decided to check around in the dresser drawers where I found them...*a lighter? No...matches, if anything they would have had to have matches at least.*

I reach my hand around the back of the top drawer, nothing. The second drawer, just some papers but what good is paper if I have no fire to put them into? I reached for a side drawer; it was smaller so it would have more promise at least that is what I had learned in my experience. I reached in, almost expecting to be disappointed when my fingers slipped over a small box: I grip it with my thumb and index finger and pull it out. To my delight it was in fact a matchbox, faded writing and a picture on the front reminded me of how long this place had been empty or at least how long someone had been holding onto the match box. I shook it first as to save myself the pain of having to see there was nothing there with my eyes, but I would only be disappointed in being wrong. Only three, but all I'd need is one. I struck it against the side and put it to the candle, not enough wick: so I tossed it into the bucket so that it could at least severe some function in the make shift fire place. I reached to grab the second candle, which was less used. Match number two, put it to the wick and to my relief had something to help get me through the night.

I began to wonder as I sat on the couch tossing a few of the papers I had found into the bucket to feed my fire, *what else do I remember?* Then I paused at the thought of trying to remember because I no longer had an audience. There was only me to retell and listen to the story. I took a deep breath, thought of what I had already said and again began to smile.

I am the only one that needs to hear I suppose, after all it is my story.

I closed my eyes and smiled at the idea of how most times, my natural audience would congratulate me after playing a game so well. Then I would put one hand in the water and feel the calm it released and I sat there, seemingly floating on top of the water and being carried away. My mind was cleared and my heartbeat was instantaneously quieted. I sat and remembered the game I had played. I remembered the sound of the water I had not seen in a long time and I remembered the true meaning of harmony. Now I knew this was not a memory invoked simply to reminisce of how to play and laugh. I was meant to allow myself to be relaxed and solidify my somewhat rickety foundation. There were no thoughts to forget because they were all being released, let go of as they were meant to be. I realized that above anything else, it was me I remembered the most, it was me I was learning to let go of.

"Trying to hold onto who I thought I should be and how I thought I should be created a nightmare. I cannot find who I am in the constant bombardment of questions because it is not enough. I should remember to let go of what I think I know when I begin to feel overwhelmed, that way I can remember the surprising simplicity I found when all I had to satisfy was my sense of adventure."

Who I am is a reflection of what I've done. What I've done has happened because of where I've been. My history has brought me to my present and the present guides me forward. It was this thought that helped me understand what I should remember.

I thought of the sky's hands coming onto my shoulders; the sun would close its eyes and bow its head in acknowledgement of my understanding. I'd look back at the stone pathway and see that the water was pointing me in a direction, when really I thought it was just going with the flow. I would think we would all just have fun and play as we did when we were younger, but I see it was only a lure towards transcendental reflection. I would applaud them and

31

all their sneaky but witty work, and before leaving the four of us would sit in silence knowing we had accomplished so much.

I took a deep breath and dipped both of my hands into the water; this was not something I had done in that time but rather something I imagined I would have done had I been there now. I would rub them together, put them in once more but this time I'd rub the water onto my forearms, then onto my face. As it slowly dripped down my face and arms, I felt it, all of it, washing away my guilt and fear. I was not recollecting a physical awakening; I was witnessing my own mental arousing, the development of my soul and expanding of my spirit. For now I knew, I could not only acknowledge my many thoughts, but I could control them.

I began to think of my past, of my future and of my present. Then I was there, here and then, it was all me. These thoughts would be the catalyst for what I would allow myself to know and understand next.

I had no intention of understanding; I just wanted to open up to new friends. Before I knew it, I was endowed with memories my spirit had been keeping to itself, the memories that had made me who I am.

Even the bad thoughts I welcomed, although it wasn't easy, I accepted them nonetheless. The harsh, the nearly nightmarish yet circumstantial pieces of my past that drove me to insanity and out into sanity shortly thereafter; as a child not only was this a place of wonder for me but also a place a refuge, my sanctuary. A world in which I could escape to, when the one I was born into became overbearing and unkind.

It is my fault I lost sight of my memories. I taught myself to hide too well from what I could not face, and so what I could not face eventually became false to me.

It was like, being lost, in a world full of opportunities for both those around me and myself. I could gaze in wonder at the future but was tragically tethered to my past, to be part of a struggle. A struggle, that no matter how hard I tried or what I did, the outcome of which was never going to be what I wanted. While I was off trying to postpone my own deterioration, others were suffering in my place.

It's all beginning to come back to me... *I remember the beginning. I remember who I am but most importantly, I remember what I know.*

As I lay my head down I was hit with another thought.

Sometimes the things we have witnessed, whatever it is we might know, can be a burden, especially if they have always been depicted as harmless and normal.

I lay there watching the flickering of the fire, with each small burst of light my eyes blinked. My chest grew warm and what I hoped was my last thought filtered through my mind. *I have to be careful. I have to make sure I don't let the flames get out of control. Each tiny ember holds in it great potential, deadly and lethal potential; just like calculated actions of misguided people...*

Pain

I was trying my best not to fight my fatigue; maybe that was what was keeping me awake, the battle to stop the battle between my mind and myself. I could once again measure the momentum of memories and the very reason why memories hold such importance. They not only allow us to remember the little things about ourselves that need be emphasized, they also give us insight into the over looked exact nature of why we are here. The things we must endure, the small things that hold the greatest of impacts for all of us, whether they are good or bad.

The truth about where I had once been and what I had come to afterward was an example I had forgotten of ache's deception in its most extensive form.

Pain occurs because of the past. It does not matter where someone is from or where he or she intends to be, pain has had a hand in shaping where they presently stand.

This recognition came as I let out a slow exhale trying hard to allow myself to rest. That was my only goal. Still, I couldn't help but wonder what it would have taken for change to happen, what would it have taken for us all to understand?

My attention was briefly brought back to the book, its unknown substances prodding at my mind.

No, not now, I don't need to think about that book now. I just want to rest. Hopefully have a good dream this time.

I began to place the blame for my pain on it, in it.

How is it one book, nothing more than pages filled with words, how is it such a thing can cause me to feel so detached? Why is it this thing can cause me to be so annoyed when it projects such obligated beginnings?

"It is a disease, this curiosity of mine. It always has been and I suppose it always will be. I know what I want but I am intimidated by what I might see while trying to get what I want. Or, what if, once I get there I find that what I thought I wanted was nothing and that all I have wanted was an illusion? Would I still then be considered crazy? Is it so crazy to simply hope for something more when all I have been told is that nothing matters?"

That makes no sense.

"If nothing matters yet I have always had this urge to be granted more then, what is it I am truly seeking? Some sense of self worth, or perhaps it's simpler than that. Maybe wanting to find something with any kind of worth, anything worthwhile is the point. If so then why is it hope has become so hurtful in this conquest that so many before me have ventured on?"

History showed us exactly what to avoid but oddly those are the lessons we chose to ignore. All we came to know was pain, being influenced to inflict it on others and ourselves because it was our common ground, our only common ground. So, the idea that was depicted as our mission of change and prosperity turned out to be our social death. Our defiance was the burden that brought on conflict. Conflicting precedents of solitude and companionship were the problem, obstacles that appeared in darkness, darkness that we initiated: We, the blinded fools, hesitant to move, with indecisive yelling in opposite directions only adding to the conundrum. Within us all, two characters sit internally begging for a resolve to be reached: our hearts, the stubborn voice and our minds, the selfish brute, their dissatisfaction intensifying over time, with no answer ever seeming to calm them.

"Nothing but disagreement and divergence based on the notion that time was in abundance. We could not see past our own quarrels to the real issues, conceit and self-satisfaction were our only ambition. We wasted time," I howled as I stood up and rubbed my hands over my eyes, out of some sort of desperation but I knew it was more than likely exhaustion.

The darkness of the room became eerily reminiscent of my own undistinguished darkened outlook. It was late at night-I knew that much-but what time, I could not say. Outside I could see flashes of light every so often; I hadn't even noticed it had started to rain. Usually I would hear the rain and appreciate it as being a sign of purification, but to me this was not a typical rain. The smell that came with it did not bring comfort. Instead, it hinted at turmoil of which I knew I would fall victim to.

It was all there, the whole time, just waiting for us to notice.

I hated my mind, loathed it for its constant inquisitions, yet as I began to think about my time as a child in my favorite place, where the hill and sun seemed to collide perfectly, I understood.

"That was always only momentary. Because at one point or another I knew I would have to go back to the truth."

I would have to leave all my bliss in that one spot and become once again, something less then delighted.

That was the difference, knowingly getting used to not being where and who I wanted.

Self torment and ridicule were my ways of coping with what I feared I would lose, endless harassment because I had to hurt so others would accept me as one of them and not see me as "the Outsider."

Therein lay the tragedy, to have wanted so badly to fit in that we compromised our own worth and sanity to do so.

An idea that had been vastly spread over hundreds of years of time was, if a person is not feeling hurt or let down in life, then life is being lived incorrectly. Our innate passion for wanting to be accepted and fit in and not be seen as "different," was the reason this message continued to spread, out of fear.

Making a difference became seen as an unmitigated lie.

"It could best be compared to being in the dark. Being in the dark stuck in some kind of wilderness and pretending to know which way to go. No matter how long you walk or how determined a person is, walking in the wrong direction will always be walking in the wrong direction. Dark or light, it doesn't matter because the choice has been made."

The only real truth that we allowed to thrive was fear and in that fear we allowed ourselves to grasp an ironic hand of death.

"We all made seemingly selfless sacrifices but in reality, they were simply unnecessary."

I should know. I slowly rose up and stepped off of the couch, walking uncomfortably toward the window.

"Why does it need to be dark? I can see everything with each lightning strike then nothing. Not one hint as to what awaits. No sign as to what is headed my way."

In my angst I had grown unsatisfied with a past I was never really a part of. It was not mine to judge, it was not mine to haul onto my shoulders and perhaps that is what annoyed me. The scent of hope in a now hopeless situation yet I still held onto it.

"It's much too late for anything to be done about things that have already happened. So then, why is it I hope to see an unseen clue as if the solution lay in my hands? I cannot be blamed for the misfortunes handed down to me. Yet still again, I have a hope that something can change them. That if I were to see their origin, even if it was something that happened a long time ago, then maybe it will help change what is now regrettably mine. Maybe…"

The other side of me seemed to disagree; the more incapable side seemed to think I was wrong.

There is nothing I can do. There is no begging or pleading with what has happened, it has been done. I was granted no say in what has become of this world but I am forced to live in it. No, I am constantly reminded of how others failed to function in it. So really, hope was something that was only heard and not seen. To have been granted hope meant that ache and pain would soon follow.

I didn't want to trust that this was all there was, I did not want this to be all that ever was suppose to be.

"The difference between living and surviving is a small margin but one step in either direction can change everything. It was not enough to try to survive as many things were lost and living came at a very high price, what happened to the middle ground?"

Then I remember seeing posters, placards and signs all with the same message, "A functional human being is a working human being."

Later on someone new decided that the term "human being" was too empowering and instead changed these words to world. That didn't last long so they decided to design an entirely new saying to feed into our minds, "If the world is to continue to function, then we must all continue to work."

It became unethical to live to be happy. It became inconceivable for any people to commit to something bigger than themselves, even though day in and day out leaders and influential groups would claim they themselves did.

With each passing day, each passing year and eventually with each passing breath we all took one more step into darkness. Neglecting the voice inside that was warning us of what was ahead. There were moments of clarity and peace, flashes of light but those were short lived. We seemed to only focus on the dark that would follow. That light came in the shape of people, of ideas and as un-metaphoric clear skies, but it was always smothered because learning to adapt and change was said to be the reason everything had become so bad for all of us in the first place.

We don't really remember those...the people are not seen as a group of individuals, they are seen as unfortunate losses. Ideas rekindled in darkness meant to help lead us back to where we began are seen as failures because they did not give us answers fast enough. They did not produce what we have convinced ourselves we want and deserve so they were discarded. In our lost state of being, we did not take the time to simply turn around when the darkness was hidden by daylight. We did not take the time to stop and think of what might be behind us because we assumed we knew the answer. We had walked from what we left behind us, walked in search of the complete solution.

At times we may have even sped up in an attempt to outrun a traumatic experience we had caused. Running from some form of uncertainty thinking, "fleeing from uncertainty is better than facing uncertainty." All we focused on was the bad; we built our history on the basis of obliterating any further harm to ourselves.

"We live in fear and die in regret. Perhaps it has always been death we have had in common; death is what we had pretended to accept. So, thinking we knew everything about an eternal nothing, we took it for granted."

We used it as an excuse to harm one another, admitting to ourselves, "Everybody dies eventually, because life is a war zone and all war zones have casualties." Statements such as these would become the cause of further self-destruction. We thought we knew that death was painful; we thought we comprehended the reason for our existence. We merely imagined our triumph, for the reality was greater than we could ever know.

There were once thriving people, communities but now what resides of them all is memories. Not just in one place but all over the world, ruins of the fallen inhabitants that seemed so sure they would not fail. Yet, as death became the most widely accepted of realities, said places became the victims of their own arrogance. As it was once agreed that death was painful to only the deceased, the departed, the living inhabitants of the world need not bother themselves with the worry of what would come. To us death seemed swift, coming and going in the swoop of a breath.

Even in this we were proven wrong.

The wind began to pick up outside, I could hear it howling, begging to be let in. The rain falling heavily against the window desperately trying to disturb what small comfort I had somehow managed to obtain.

A funny thing about the rain, at times it may seem friendly and light but most often it only cares about itself. Doing only what it thinks it should do based on the influences around it. I thought to myself and recognized *we are often like the rain. Falling and following no path but that which we are pushed or pulled into.*

"I suppose, if not for the influences of outer sources, all we would ever do or have done was fall." There I stood, straining to make out raindrops just before they broke against the window.

"Then again, the forces that have often seemed to capture us in a moment were really catching up to us tolerantly overtime."

It seems as though we have always been incomprehensible specks falling towards some unknown destination and only when outside forces presume to give us some sort of direction do we think we have stopped our true nature.

What I had come to understand based on the few times I had witnessed death is that it is not swift, nor is it easy to be taken in death, to lose something once believed to be the right of an individual.

Our only right is to live and to influence others to do the same.

"Yet again as we walked through an everlasting shadow we did not take the time to fathom the deadly shape of our own. The tattered skin, the chaotic tears, the apprehensive smile and hands and feet soaked in blood. As we walked, we trod over ourselves not stopping to help or see what direction the broken bodies lay. We maintained that all of us, in the end, die no matter what and used this to justify not filling our empty lives. We expected to believe in what had been brought to our attention through ambiguity rather than believe in the inconsolable reflections that were all around us."

There was not only anguish in our past but lessons to be learned, as most of what we feared had been self-inflicted. In the very spot from which we began our trudge were two solutions. Not meant to be marveled at for days at a time or to have one seen as more important than the other. Rather, to be acknowledged as a pair and seen as equals.

It was just the rain and me now. I did not notice the flashes of light and I did not notice the darkness of the room.

"Just you and me, face to face."

I should know.

"I should know you as I have seen you numerous times in my life."

I should know.

"I should know what it is you will push me to understand but I should also know that you only hold one half of a torn picture."

I should know…

"That you and I are a pair, we are equals. I have never tried to outshine you but you have often forced yourself into my state of being."

Again I could see my faint reflection in the window, drops of rain hitting hard in order to infiltrate the illusion.

"It is interesting to see you from this perspective. To be on the inside where I guess, is where you usually are. You fall and plunder into my persona and have no care of what you cause. I know my control over you is an illusion, I know that you and I have had numerous confrontations that resulted in my dissatisfaction. I ask you, why? What was the point in going through such a horrendous affair?"

Maybe, this is the point? This point right here where I stand and you fall, aimlessly wanting me to join you.

"You are no more better at falling than I am at standing. We may both start out with stubborn determination but in the end we are equals, tired and brought down by our own disgrace."

I should know.

"I have been doing it for a long time now. This is not me proposing a truce simply because I know that would not be in your character, no. Instead I offer you comfort, the same comfort you have granted me. You may do what you wish but I will not stop and will not quit simply because it is inconvenient for you."

I turned away and could not help but smile, not because I knew I had won a long-standing battle. I smiled because I knew that the pain of the past and future was a storm I would just have to get through. The rain this night did not let up, yet I was able to forget about it completely. I knew that because of this unknown shelter I had stumbled upon, I was safe from a familiar foe. It had granted me new senses or possibly just re-opened old ones. Either way the smile on my face was the acknowledgement of the shelter arranged by uncertainty. For that, in this very moment, I was content.

Life and living do not go hand in hand, this had often been the common misconception. Life is the essence of all things and all things share life. Living was defined as capturing a memory or stealing a moment. Living was said to be the product of one person's obligations toward him or herself. In truth, living is something we have been made to do together. Just as we must all eat or drink or breath, so did we need to learn to live, out of necessity. Death, all the while, is slow, patient and unforgiving. It does not care for preparation nor does it heed to the rules of time. From the moment we are born, Death is not far behind waiting for the slightest hint of irresponsibility so that it may remind those around us what ignorance costs. Still, that was our source of pride, ignorance.

Within death, only then do we recognize beauty, we embellish each and every instance as it is given to us but still, in our haste-in our, greed-death became irrelevant and only promiscuous and pointless victories became prominent. Our veins pulsated with devastating longing, we relished in causing the chaos of others but most entertained of all ideas was the thought of seeing ourselves on top of our fellow human beings. The insatiable want to prove who was the best was not accomplished by all of us but by one of us, or a small group of us.

Here my mind and heart found common ground but this did not ease me as I imagined it would. I could feel the two beginning to cooperate but the thought of living in such a world where the claim of an idea was much greater than the idea itself could ever be made me feel, something familiar. There was a burning, a grueling and fretful feeling. I was not certain if what I was feeling was the very thing those before me, who had allowed such atrocities, had felt just before they inexplicitly unleashed pain onto themselves. I was, I was angry, I was sad, I was hurt and the only thing I could bring myself to say again was, "how could we allow such a thing to happen?"

Just, how?

This propelled me to get up again, I was pacing, in my mind I was running; running to reach anything and everything that I saw enter my mind while trying my best not to stumble.

How? How did we go from having such great potential to wanting nothing more than to harm one another? How is it, individuals were produced over time only to be struck down by the excuse that, "The world was not ready for change?" How, how could so much destruction be allowed while care and understanding were given no second thought?

Inside, I was burning, feverish with self-guilt and angst. Trembling out of disappointment, *no, not disappointment,* I was trembling because I had grown cold. In all my movement I had somehow started to snuff my fire, it was beginning to dwindle down. I had become too distracted, in my search for our lost societies apathy, to notice. I fed it with a few more bits of paper, taking a seat back on the couch folding my arms across my chest reminding myself I would have to keep an eye on the fire until I was able to rest.

Can I rest?

I could not help but think of the pointless persecutions we claimed were our right to bestow onto others. In any way we were able to think of, we destroyed the worlds of others all because we felt our world and their world were vastly different. There was no emotion in our tone of reckoning, no empathy within our visions of dismay. We felt obligated to pursue the slaughter of uncharted ideals.

A man could be without a woman, but a woman without a man was worth less than nothing. A child was deprived of innocence if they chose to believe in something more than what they could see. A family that was forced to live with nothing was still forced to give up everything, when their child was called to help wage war. A broken heart was not often fixed in the ways it should have been; but a jaded mind was always fed and well nourished. Certain images were depicted as perfection while the truth of a person's body image was seen with disgust. Wealth became the source for determining what a person should receive but what we had become accustom to seeing as wealth, not soon after was acknowledged as destitution.

What was once an inclination of prosperity, soon after became the very definition of poverty not just for a select few, for all. Like a stillborn baby to an anxious set of parents, an opportunity for the best of miracles had become the worst of circumstances. All of us attempting to grasp what we could only hope had been a nightmare, hopelessly gasping for air in an attempt to wake ourselves. Hands stretched out in desperation wishing, wanting, and waiting to be pulled back to, just before, the sudden moment of despair.

We all knew there was no going back, because what we left behind were lessons to be remembered, as history.

We would rather suffer and wallow in the angst of where we had been instead of move forward with caution due to experiences we had gotten through together. It had taken us numerous decades to realize how to admit our faults on a worldwide level; our own imperfections had been put on display but still we seemed to thrive on discomfort. On our own, yes but unfortunately more so on the agony of those around us as it was implicated to deny, whomever, of anything and everything we all deeply yearned for.

I could only ask myself, "How did we do it? I have gone from having no will to live, to being determined to succeed..."

That was my triumph, but what is one person's triumph amidst a world focused on failures?

"No rest will be granted to me tonight, not when my mind has been persuaded by the unrest of the past."

Unfortunately, this had become a kind of routine; a tediously provocative occurrence and I still had yet to figure out why. Why I had come to this place, how is it I could feel distress for things I had not been around to witness?

Perhaps, in the quick and brutal action of wanting to claim victory, only more had been lost. More of what was needed was buried as a result of the desire for less precious commodities.

The only thing I could think to have happened, the only thing I was able to understand was:

We killed each other, slowly but surely. In our haste to reach the top, we failed to help those who struggled down below. We assumed it was a one-person climb; only one could make it to the top in order to represent us all but, none of us stopped to think of what was really going on. As a few of us hastily made our way up we did not realize we were crushing those beneath us. We did not realize the reason the top seemed so far away was because we had never gotten more than a few feet off the ground. Those below were not being used to push off of; they had been used as a pathway. They were beginning to buckle under our feet and if we fell we would not land on our feet but rather, we would be buried beneath them. As many continued to jump and attempt to climb up, the people they thought had no purpose would decay at their feet unable to help them achieve their false victory. Soon all would become known as the unacknowledged.

"We have never been made to succeed on our own, we were made and placed here to help one another achieve clarity and truth. We are not meant to ascend up with out the help of others."

So had those on top simply reached down and grabbed the hands of those struggling beneath them, then no one would be left to wallow in agony, grief and despair. No one person or group of people is meant to come out of life untouched, if we had been able to live properly then as we reached the top we would all be able to acknowledge the wear and tear made on our hands from the climb up. What pains me the most is, knowing there is nothing I can do about it now.

"If only this simple thing had been done, if only this miniscule task had been perceived, so many could have been saved but more so, so much time could have been spared and spent on greater things." I stood in silence, feeling powerless and ashamed.

Outside, there was the wind and the rain: inside, a somewhat still burning candle and a bucket of fire. A small, poorly kept bucket and what was I to expect? No one had been here for a long time now; no one was going to bother keeping anything in this place and why should they? What is the significance of a forgotten home to a person who does not understand what a home should be?

"Why should I even care of what this place looks like or feels like? What is there to stop me, from tearing everything apart and setting fire to it all? Sure the rain would most likely stop it from spreading but in here there would be no hope. Nothing for anyone else to find or use or claim for their own selfish needs." I stopped and briefly contemplated the consequences.

Could I actually do it? Would I truly be able to tip the bucket and walk away knowing absolutely nothing would be left? And, what of the raindrops? In my exasperated focus, they would be forced to make haste and their gentle and steady fall would then turn into an expedient yet pointless execution of saving this forgotten place.

Outside I could hear the small taps of rain hitting the window, countless drops falling. I wondered if the drops raced each other from the sky, each one trying its hardest to fall before any of the others.

No, raindrops do not race to see which one is best, nor do they have a desire to prove so. They simply fall, freely and without concern because they know it may be the only chance they have to enjoy what little time they are given. The possibility of a collision with a fellow raindrop is a privilege, if and when it may happen, otherwise they know they do not need to obsess over such a thing in order to complete their purpose.

It is in this overlooked of occurrences that rain helped me understand in that one night, what many before me could not understand in decades and lifetimes.

If all we ever allow ourselves to know is pain, then how can we ever expect to benefit? Benefit from all we have come to know and the many things we still struggle to understand.

However, that is all we had done for a long time. Focused on the pain caused by others wishing to only in return, cause pain to them along with the many others who seemed to "get in our way."

That is how we died.

"Our mistake was thinking we knew what our mistake was."

The rain had begun to slow to a drizzle and the wind had died down or perhaps, it had simply moved on.

"We thought we could out think the collective of our minds. We tried desperately to tip the scale in our favor as to out weigh the repercussions of our insensitive logic. We were wrong, on the grandest of scales."

I looked down at the fire as I threw in half of my remaining pile of papers. I was warm but it was no longer tiring and conspiratorial warmth from within me, the fire was keeping me warm and I knew I had again begun to relax. I looked over at the candle, a quarter of the way from being burned out.

"You will be getting tossed in here soon my friend, but I promise it is not out of hatred, simple necessity I assure you."

How odd that I would reassure the candle of its death so easily; odder still that I had grown to care for such a thing as a nearly dead candle. After all, I was just using it for exactly what it was meant for. To be burned away, lit and then extinguished by its own hand. All candles are made with only a certain length of wick, after that their purpose was complete.

But to think, think of all the things they are part of in their short life. All the things they can inspire and the small bit of light that can make all the difference in the most unsettling darkness. They probably care less about what will happen to them than what they help to accomplish.

"Maybe candles don't burn out, it is also possible that they burn up. They reach towards a point higher than themselves because they can. They glow because they must but when they die, they die for a reason."

I could see the candle start to fade and I started to feel the weight of what it might have gone through before gasping for its last bits of oxygen. I tried to time my breathing to the wick's steady puffs.

"Big breath, slow exhale; big breath, slow exhale. Big breath…slow exhale…*yawn*…Big breath in…"

Love

How long I was asleep I am not quite sure but I woke up feeling both rested and somewhat rejuvinated. It was no longer raining. but the window was still wet from when it had been.

"I guess it has been a few hours. At least I would imagine so."

I stood and stretched and while doing so let out a yawn, *always a sign of a restful sleep.*

A quick walk to the window as I continued to stretch, to gage what time it might be now.

It's dark out but there is light beginning to come through in the distance. It might be around early morning.

I stood near the couch before beginning to clean up the bits of ash from the fire, and then my stomach began to grumble. I had been so focused on calming myself down and putting my mind at ease that I had not thought to look for anything to eat. I know I didn't have anything on me, well unless I counted a quarter loaf of bread as a meal.

"No. Not today. I feel I will need much more than that, I just hope there is something for me to eat here. Although this place has provided a few surprises so far, I don't see why it wouldn't deliver with something to eat as well."

Hope. I gave a slight smile with this simple word of a thought because for the first time since I could remember, I said it in a sentence without feeling any sense of regret afterwards.

Hmm, interesting.

I made my way toward the kitchen, passing the table where the book lay right in the middle on top of my jacket. Even though I noticed it, it didn't seem to bother me as much as it had the night before. It could have been that I was too hungry to notice or that I just had more patience in regards to its presence or maybe both. Either way, it was a good feeling, not to let something effect my mood in a negative way.

I don't remember the last time I wasn't thinking about my mood and need or wanting to change it out of fear. Come to think of it, I don't remember the last time I felt just, rested and aware or level headed. Well, maybe I am not completely leveled out but at least I am getting there.

I knew my best chances of finding anything to eat would come from the cabinets or the refridgerator. I walked to the refrigerator and realized as I did that it was standing right next to a plug in the wall. I looked at the back of it and saw that the cord had been pulled out of it. "So much for that."

55

Now the question is, will the cabinets be willing to help me or would they instead shun my needs because I did so to them when I first came in? I wouldn't blame them really. It would be nice though if they were not the type of things to hold a grudge.

I looked in each one. *One, nothing. Two: a small spoon and a can opener. Three, nothing. Four...*

There was some canned food. Three cans. Some kind of vegistable mix, a fruit cocktail and beans. No labels on either of them, instead each one's contents were written on the top in black marker. It wasn't an odd thing to not see labels on can foods, there hadn't been a canned food company around in many years.

As grateful as I was to have something to eat, I couldn't help but look at the can of beans and feel a bit let down. *Of course, if anything there would be beans here. I am too hungry to be picky though.*

When I was younger, the people I lived with had beans with everything. Even with their sweets. There were always beans. I was happy to have something to eat but as soon as I grew up and was given the chance to venture out on my own, I promised myself I would never eat beans again. So of course, here they were. In any other time, at any other point in my life I would be miserable having them near me but in this moment, I was greatful.

Life has found another way to bring something from the past full circle. I am surprised about this, I guess I shouldn't be at this point. Often we, I, have or will want something and expect it to be as I imagine only to be most of the time handed the reality of not knowing that need overshadows want. I may want to have something but I will most likely need something else. I wanted food and was instead given compact meal sides, one of which mocks my taste pallet's past with it's unveiling. I at one time wanted to find only my purpose and was instead granted numerous defining moments in my life. It is, afterall, human nature to want something we do not know but think we do. To ask others for something we only need for ourselves. We hear something and think it to have truth to it, a small part in most cases but even that small truth gives us reason to somehow validate a lie. Then another small lie is blended in with truth and then aother and then another, then before we could do anything about it, lies began to exstiguish the truths we took for granted. The truths I took for granted.

The truth has always been a natural occurance. The resource that flourished even when no one could know it exsisted. Over time though, it became burdened and burried beneath miniscule lies. Such tiny lies that none thought to pay too much attention to. Then they grew, and grew and slowly took over, like a virus. A virus not only handed down from generation to generation but one that grew in capacity with each new dawning. The truth began to be the thing we hated, the thing we feared just because we lost sight of the right matter in wrong matters.

As I looked down at the three cans of food, as I stared at the bean can, I couldn't help but think, *How great it is to see you, now.*

Despite my spite towards you for just being as you are, you are here willing to nourish me. You may not be delicious or a feast of feasts but I have somehow found my way back to you. Odder still is the fact that now I feel more at home just having you right in front of me. I guess without you, I never would have left in the first place...Maybe I should thank you, for all you have allowed me to know and understand without you in my life. I know much more about who I am now because of where I have been and gone and I love how it has worked out that here you are once more. As if I had never been without a home.

Silence was all around me. Early morning silence, the kind that seems to only allow movement with each breath taken by the select few who choose to view its happening. The silence that seems loudest because sincere sounds are accomplished and unpolluted by the negation of the morning's arrival. I sat the cans on the table, put my jacket on the couch and placed the book right next to it, I still couldn't help but feel there was a connection between the book and myself.

I went back to the second cabinet for the small spoon and can opener. A quick spit shine on the spoon with help of my shirt to wipe it off, opened the cans and took out my piece of bread. One small bite of each first to be sure they were still good. *Didn't taste too bad,* I thought. I had to remind myself to pace the meal despite how hungry I felt. I sat back in the chair after eating the vegistables and half the can of fruit.

"Love," I said. I said it again but in a whisper. "Love…"

An illusion to some, a fable to others, but still anyone and everyone have and had heard about it. So, what happened? Where does it begin? Where did it end? Can it ever trully end?

Was love something that had been here since the beginning or did it evolve as life evolved, into a force that still goes on unexplained? Is it a simple connection or is it a series of connections formulated over time to give the illusion of a simple connection? Do we desire it because it is unknonwn or does it remain to be labled as unknown because we think it is something we have to understand in order to obtain?

Maybe all we are suppose to do with love is accept it, appreciate it. Allow it to be part of our lives, allow it to live in who we are and what we do. Maybe that is where it began, with us, from our beginning. Maybe love was our first triumph as human beings, our only widely known triumph as human beings. Maybe all we have and will ever try to do is get back to that same feeling of victory, the very first feeling of accomplishment with things we think stand at the same level as love. Subconciously knowing there is no such thing that can match the truth and strength of love but consciously trying to overthrow our better judgement.

"On the opposite end of it, what if love was our only great acheivment? What if we have been trying to best our own greatness in the opposite direction of our origin point? Creating a class of better and best bcause we have forgotten how to stand together."

In pursuit of becoming better in numerous individual markets, we have allowed our true potential to fall behind. It lingers in our past, waiting for us to realize we left it behind and make our way back to retrieve it.

"If we created love, then why have we allowed ourselves to fail to keep it going?" I finished half of my beans and set the rest aside. I took a bite of bread as I reached for the vegistable mix.

"Nourishment…" I said.

"Love is meant to nourish us. It is nourishment for the weaker parts of who we are or who we are afraid to be."

Can that be true? Could the result of our denial of love's luminance be caused by the lack of soulful nutrition? Have we grown to strive more towards power in hopes of boosting our pride that we have made love out to be the losers reward?

"Love is meant to lift the fallen and humble those who feel they are at their peaks. Love sees no color nor sense of wealth, in the pressence of love everything matters." The sun began to show through the window slightly more. It was gaining warmth and hieght as was I.

"Love grants wisdom when ignorance seems to be all that is left. It shows courage when fear and doubt have grown out of control and it brings peace when only small pieces of positivity remain."

Yet, to acknowledge love is to admit weakness. To indulge love is to cater to the inferior parts of society because only the ignorant can love.

"At least, that is what we were told."

59

Told no from the beginning and then over and over again through a serises of small lies exchanged in stories and tales all ensighting love as the wrong thing to desire. Much of them were derived from history, our history, our greatest fault to counter our greatest acheivment.

"This very way of thinking has brought us all to this point." I looked down at the other half of beans in the can and saw them as the other half of my own misguided history.

"As much of a pain as you are to eat all at one time, I can't believe how much you have taught me in the short time we have been reuinited. You are part of my dissatisfaction, you are a piece of things I have tried long to forget yet I cannot deny the fact that you are a piece of me. A small portion of who I am and who I have become.

"An odd side dish you are, beans, yet you can be put together with so many different meals from numerous places around the world. In each place you hold a certain value, some places value you more than others and most places have at one point or another taken you for granted."

Nevertheless they are part of the entire world's history. Perhaps it was a bit of beans that enduced the first outward expression of love. When a family sat and ate from a pile of beans on a rainy night in a cave, all they had were beans but those beans brought them together and somehow without speaking a word they knew what love was. They may not have known quite what it could be but they knew it was something special. For all of them to be together when elements and a changing world around them could have torn them apart.

"Here I am, someone who once cmplained about getting too many beans on my plate, eating an entire can to myself because I have begun to understand what that one family figured out in a night.

Love does not care what we have, love is meant to show us what is real."

Is it ironic or poetic that, if that were to be how it happened, I would be eating the same meal as that family as I relearn the most basic of truths? To be able to connect to a past so far beyond mine even if it were not true, the fact of knowing how far back the beginning was is astonishing in itself. To establish a connection in any way is to accept a deeper part of who a person really is and can be.

"I suppose it makes sense that love would have begun with a sense of fullfilling a basic need. For a people of any origin to gather around a meal and know in just a few short moments, why it is they are who they are and doing what they are doing."

I scooped the last bit of beans onto a corner piece of bread and with that, they were gone. All I had left to enjoy was the rest of the fruit cocktail. I had always been a fan a fruit and opeining up the can. I knew this part of the meal would be very short lived. I sat back in the chair and just obsevered, watched as the sun began to kiss the top of a different building with every inch it rose. Every so often it would lighlty touch the tops of piles of rubble.

I had been awoken by many a sunrise but always against my will and there I sat peering out at one. Feeling as though I had made the sun hasten its routine in order to keep up with my accidental timely manner.

"Good day sir, I see I beat you to the morning."

I ate the rest of my fruit surprisingly slow, slurping one to two pieces of fruit at a time as I watched to see what else might be uncovered as the sun continued it's climb towards its post in the sky.

Understanding

I poured the last quarter of the syrup from the bottom of the can into my mouth. That had always been my favorite part, even though other people found it gross. I washed it out in the sink and set it on the counter next to my two other empty canned meals. I stood, leaning against the windowsill just looking out. Just letting my eyes wander, curiously scanning for any kind of clue to something new.

It was just around mid-morning and the streets had begun to come more and more alive. "Has it always been like this, have I been too trapped in my own thoughts to notice?" There was a stray dog, wandering around to a few shops that seemed to know it and welcomed it with a good morning treat.

"Now, that is not a bad way to spend a morning. At least morning meals are a guarantee for her...or him...for it."

One of the shop owners was standing outside her store stretching and getting ready for the day. Another was just sitting in an old kitchen chair out front staring at the horizon. There were a few kids dashing in between trees and piles or rubble, and it seemed as though they were pretending to be part of a hunt of some kind. Then I saw their prey, the man sitting in the chair looking the other way.

"Are they going to knock him down, or attack him? What kind of a game is this?"

They crept closer and closer and closer and then, just before they pounced, the man spun around and whipped out a shield. It looked to be an old trashcan lid with the logo of an old comic book hero on it.

"I wonder who will win, or who has won the most because it seems like this is a pretty normal routine for all of them."

I closed my eyes and I could feel the warmth of the sun come over me. Something new was going to happen, something different, I could tell.

I began to feel anxious, restless in my surroundings. I had this sense of discovery going through me and I could feel it pushing me, persuading me to step outside of my newly established barriers. I wasn't afraid but more so, intimidated by my own desire to give in to this feeling. I didn't know what would happen or where I would go but I think at that moment I realized that it was okay to not fully know something.

"What is the worst that can happen? I mean I came to rest here by accident. I just wandered up here and it just happened to work in my favor. Now the only difference from then to now is the time that has passed."

I stood and stretched for a moment feeling good in my decision. Then I grabbed my jacket, put the last bit of bread into one of the outer pockets and stopped. There it was just sitting on the couch, the book, with its blank front and back cover just like in my dream.

What do I do with you? Should I leave you and come back for you later or take you with me? I stood for a moment, thinking, looking out at the kids and the man playing their game.

You know what? I don't know if I will come back, I don't really know where I will go when I leave so I think I have to take you with me. You will be a good reminder of what I have been a part of here and a good change of pace from my other pocket inhabitants. You may even provide me with good entertainment at some point.

I threw on my jacket, put the book in the other outer pocket and then zipped it up. I took a few steps toward the door and just as I reached for the handle I looked back, so I could get one more look at everything that was there. One final look at the hours that had passed and see the different parts of me I had uncovered. It was a strange feeling, as if I were leaving bits of me behind for the next person to find or for the next day and night to collect into their stream of events and truths.

"Thank you, for your help and for allowing me to help you," I said as I shut the door behind me.

As I came down the stairs, I got a whiff of this morning's breath. It held in it hints of fragrances from around this part of the block and slight scents of the rain from the previous night. A story was being uncovered with each inhale. I could smell flowers waiting to be admired, the smells of a breakfast being prepared and near the end of the wind was an aroma of something sweet.

When I opened the door to leave, a baker walked by me with a box full of the sweet smell. Grapes, melon, strawberries and maybe even blueberry and it took me a moment to realize what they were.

65

"Fruit tarts. Delectable, delicate and sweet but not overly so as to ruin a morning appetite. I wonder where she is going."

I closed the door behind me and then searched for keys so I could return, *No, you don't live here. You were just, visiting. If you need to come back, you know how to get here but you shouldn't worry about that just now.*

The day was calm, or at least starting off that way as it was hard to tell what could happen later on. I began to walk down the street, strolling along and trying my best to take in all that I could. A glass shop on one side that had beautiful small cups and sculptures, one configured to look as if they were dancing together. A tall golden figure held a slightly shorter light blue piece in the middle and it looked as though two ballroom dancers had been caught in glass and frozen in time, dancing to music that had been trapped in the glass with them. There were sets of oddly shaped plates, all different sizes, that were stained in numerous greens and blues and a few browns with a few red and orange and yellow.

"Oh I see. They represent the elements." I would have gone in to look at what more was there but the shop had not yet opened.

Oh well, another time. I don't have any money to spend here anyway.

I saw a bookstore across the street and wondered if they might be open.

I haven't read a book in a while and I have a bit of energy to burn, at least I think so. I don't know why considering I haven't had much sleep. Maybe a book can help with that.

"Closed. Apparently I am out at the time when shop keepers are still getting ready for the days activities."

I looked in the window, peered hard through it and when I couldn't see anything, put my face on the glass and covered the sides of it with my hands. I was hoping to see if there were any books that were a match to the one I had found. I guess, I guess I was looking for an easy escape or a short cut to what I would no doubt have to do.

There was a scream that came from my right, and then a loud groan and I heard the older man start speaking.

"No! This cannot be...I must *cough, cough* save the city from evil...I cannot fail..." And then the old man started to fall to the ground while holding his chest. He tossed the trash can lid aside and held the now free hand out, towards a building across the street. "But wait!" He said, "The hero can still call for help from his fellow super hero team. Will he get the call in time, has evil finally won, does he need a Band-Aid? Come back tomorrow to see what happens next!"

The kids turned to one another as if planning another assault, "No, no, we must conclude for today. It's nearly time to work and I see your mom over there waiting for you. Go on, that way you have time to plan for tomorrow."

"Do we have to?" A little boy and girl said in unison.

"Yes. Don't worry, tomorrow will be here before you know it, I promise."

"Tomorrow is forever away!"

"It is only forever at this moment in time but forever has a tendency of becoming yesterday faster than you think. Now go, you shouldn't keep your mother waiting."

They all scurried off, still continuing their own battles of the game.

I stepped a bit closer to see if the man needed help cleaning up his portion of the gear. "Hey there, good morning."

He was an older man but he had a young air about him. He stood at around five feet ten inches tall or so with a complexion that was only slightly darker than the pants he wore. He wore a sweater vest over his t-shirt, casual looking tan pants and a casual looking pair of dress shoes, which were black to match some of the pattern on his vest. His eyes were a light brown and his hair, a dark shade with hints of grey, looked as though it had been growing back for a few weeks after being completely shaven off. His beard stubble and goatee, also with small hints of grey hairs, enhanced his smile and the wrinkles in his cheeks suggested that he smiled quite a lot. "Good morning. Did you enjoy our little show?"

"Yes I did. How long have you been doing it?"

"What? Playing with kids? Since forever, oh no, it has been so long I am beginning to sound like them."

"It wouldn't be so bad as long as it keeps you young right?"

He laughed as he slowly bent down to pick up the trash lid and placed it on top of the can. "Yes, I suppose. Any little thing helps."

"You have quite a few little things it seems to keep you busy."

"It's a good way to start the morning. Gives me a chance to get some exercise in before I open up shop and it gives their mother a chance to prepare a good meal for all of them with out needing to stop."

"All of those kids are from one woman?"

"No, no, she has two of her own, the twins, Marco and Connie. The others she has taken in because they were abandoned or had no place else to go. I just do my part to show them that life can still be fun as long as you are willing to venture out past the bad and harsh experiences. Come inside, we can talk more while I set up if you'd like."

"Yes, thank you. Anything I can do to help?"

"Just un-stack the chairs from the tables, that should be good enough. They are heavier than they look though."

"So you said you have been doing what you do with them forever? The oldest one was maybe eight years old, right? So, how long have you looked after them every morning?"

"Actually he is nine, Jordan, and he takes his responsibility seriously. He looks after them all and took the longest to warm up to me but now, he has eased up and when they are with me in the morning, he has just as much fun as his younger siblings."

"Awe, well that's good then. And the others?"

"Well Marco and Connie like to cause a bit of trouble here and there but are really good at solving puzzles, especially together, and they are the third oldest. Between them and Jordan is Shelly. She is tiny for her age but she is quick. She can out run all the others and loves to climb in fact, that pile of rubble leading to the tree next to my roof out there, she asked me to build it for her. The girl has no fear of heights. Then there are Kevin and Ben, or little Benjamin. Kevin is going to be seven soon but he and the twins are never the same age for long and Ben just turned five. He is shy but can always tell you when someone new comes along, that is how I knew you were watching our game. Kevin and Ben are more observant, they like to watch the older kids play so they can learn all they can from them. Usually when we play a game those two are the spies or messengers or something along those lines, just because it makes it easier to sit back and spectate."

"Wow, sounds like you know them pretty well."

"Yea, well, like I said, I have been doing this forever. I had my own kids before everything went to crap and I used to play with them all the time. Then the world changed and we were separated. They were older by then but I have grand kids out there that I don't think I will ever be able to see. So, these six little hooligans are considered by me to be a gift."

"You seem very positive considering you have lost some of the ones you have held dear."

"Like I said, life can be fun despite being treated unfairly. So, what can I get for you?"

"What do you mean?"

"Well, you look tired. It is lucky for you that you are in a coffee shop. I am pretty sure I have the cure for that exhaustion you are suffering from."

"How can you tell I'm exhausted?"

"You have bags under your eyes, bags almost as heavy as my coffee bean bags."

"Oh wow, I had no idea I looked that bad. It's been, kind of a long night for me."

"Well, how about some coffee to make it easier to handle what will most likely be a long day?"

"Thank you but, I haven't got much money."

"Its alright, you don't have to pay just tell me a bit of what you have on your mind. Maybe I can help."

"...I really wouldn't know where to start."

"That's fine. I would think that the best place to start would be right now. You have the look of someone looking for something they didn't know they lost. So, what do you think that might be?"

"I think I am just looking to understand things. I have just now begun to feel aware of what I am unaware of and at the same time, I am just barley in tune with who I want to be. I just don't understand what to do with the little I have."

"I see, I see. Why, may I ask, do you see what you have as little? Here you go."

"Thank you. Because I know there is still so much more out there."

"There is always going to be more out there but it is always going to be out there. You are in here, right now, what do you have to show for it?"

"Bags under my eyes and a cup of coffee."

"Not bad, kind of obvious but it's a start. Let me tell you something, something I learned fairly recently. If someone wants to understand something, whether it is in themselves, their purpose or in the world in general, one must first learn to accept."

"Accept?"

"Yes. This is much easier said than done but I promise you, it can be done. Let me ask you something, how many times have you been wrong in your life time?"

"Well without people telling me, a lot."

"Okay and in each time you are wrong or were wrong, did you learn from that mistake?"

"Yes. Sometimes it took me a while but I did eventually learn."

"Of course you did, because you are human. It doesn't matter how long it takes you to learn the lesson, the point is that you learn the lesson. As long as your heart is in the right place it's never going to be too late to grow and get better. Progression is granted to those who are willing to be wrong."

"Isn't that really risky, I mean, isn't that how the world got to be the way it is now?"

"Yes and no. You see back then, people believed in anything and everything. Nobody bothered to check for facts or verifications and those that did were cast aside."

"I know how that feels."

"As do I. But the real problems began when we grew to ignore the obvious possibility that all of us could be wrong. We began to put all our faith into never being wrong that eventually our faith, lead to our downfall. Don't get me wrong, its important for anyone to have something to believe in. For instance, I believe one day I will see my kids and grand kids but I also understand that there is a high chance of me being wrong, and I accept that. But believing in something and forcing others to believe what you do because you fail to see similarities between what they have faith in and what you have faith in, leads to nothing but destruction both internally and externally. How we now live is an example of that."

"So chance, in your case, is your risk. You believe that you may see them again but are most likely going to be disappointed and can be proven wrong?"

"Yes. But that is my risk to take and it affects me more than it effects anyone else, unless I pour my expectations into the lives of others in which case, it becomes everybody's problem. The great thing about chances is the matter of one person taking one and being rewarded for it in a way they had not at all thought of or expected. Take you and me for example."

"You mean how I saw you playing with the kids?"

"I mean me inviting you into my shop not knowing anything about you other than you looking tired. I don't even know your name."

"Oh yea, I'm sorry. I must be tired, I hadn't thought to introduce myself."

"It's okay, me knowing your name would not have made a difference in my choice. The point is that I took a chance, that I was willing to take a chance to invite a stranger into my closed shop and was willing to experience something new."

"But you couldn't do what you did with me to anybody right? I mean you can't just invite a stranger a day to come in and expect nothing bad will happen, right?"

"You're right, and I wouldn't do something like that because that would be foolish. Chance is not based on foolishness, it is based on circumstance, there are many variables that go into chance, many things that are often over looked because chance is placed in high regards. People used to take chances with the expectation that everything would work out for them no matter what. That isn't how chance works. Chance is a cousin of logical thinking, and because of this there is no point in taking a chance if you do not first consider logical consequences."

"So you considered both the good and bad outcomes of what could happen if you let me in here?"

"Yes but I also took into account your apparent fatigue and the fact that I have been up playing with kids, getting my blood circulating, for a few hours. Now in your peak condition, yes, you could over power me but had you have tried something, you would have barely made it across the street before I caught up with you."

"You seem to know quite an awful lot about chance and risk. How do you know all this?"

73

"In the past life, I was a teacher. Knowing things was part of my job that way I could help show my students what it meant to truly learn all that life has to offer."

There was a knock on the door and that sweet smell came back to me as he walked over to open it, it was the baker, she had been making deliveries.

"Good morn-oh, hello. You have company. Shall I come back later?"

"No, its alright, I have been expecting you. Besides, the more the merrier. Running a little late today are you?"

"Well you know how it goes with Martha, once she gets talking its hard to find a way to end the conversation."

"Oh yes, I am sure I will be seeing her later on today."

"I will be back later as well, just wanted to stop by and give you your goodies for breakfast."

"Thank you. They are always a great addition to the mornings. I will see you tonight too, right?"

She giggled and kissed him on the cheek, "Of course, this time, I'll cook."

"See you later then my baker."

"I didn't realize how late it had gotten into the morning. Do you mind if we carry on this conversation another time? I need to start getting more things ready. You don't have to leave or anything. You are more than welcomed to stay even after you finish your coffee. Hopefully our talk helped you get closer to what it is you want."

"Thank you. I think it did. I am not quite sure to be honest, I will know better once the coffee kicks in I'm sure."

"That adorable woman, she always gives me more than I can eat, would you like one? Have you ever had a fruit tart?"

"Not in a long time."

Two servings of fruit in not just one day but one morning, am I being rewarded for something? If so, then thank you. This will not go unappreciated I assure you.

The sun began to rise faster, or so it seemed, and as it got higher I could feel my back getting warmer. I didn't want to take off my jacket but I also didn't want to sit there in a sweat.

Not long after he finished setting up did a couple of people come in. Both greeted him in their own way. A small lady with her hair tight in a bun came in and waved at him, put her jacket on a table and then walked up to order. She spoke politely but with a tone that suggested she was in a rush, which was odd because she only sat back down at the table and opened a book. She didn't move after she got her drink and pastry.

I wonder if the book she is reading is that good, she looks very determined.

A younger man walked in, taller than the café owner but thinner in comparison, he had on a mismatched set of pants and jacket and shoes that didn't go with either one. He had on glasses that seemed too big because he kept adjusting them each time he moved his head. He seemed frantic, but tried desperately to keep his calm. He asked for something to eat and espresso, *Are you sure you want to do that?*

After getting his espresso he sat at the table adjacent to mine but sat facing the window. He nodded at me and smiled, then at the

75

lady who smiled quite nicely at him and then immediately went right back to reading her book.

I just sat there, waiting to witness more traffic and trying to make more sense of what the owner and I had talked about. I would sip my coffee then pause and think for a while, then sip my coffee some more and go back to thinking. The fruit tart was good; it had always been one of my favorite treats. It was saddening to notice when I had picked up the last piece and know that even if I cherished that small bite, it would fade into the forgotten memory of my taste buds before I had time to lick my lips.

As I stared at the mug in my hand I couldn't help but chuckle at the thought that coffee was once seen as a luxury. Sold within a market that tried each and every day to convince so many people of what luxuries had to be.

Now we have bags and bags and pounds and pounds of it. Just to use, nobody tries to sell it and nobody tries to steal it because it wouldn't really be worth anything to anybody. It's just, a thing. Something we have, not have to have but just have around like plants. Which makes sense considering it does come from a tree.

Had this been in the past, I would be viewed as an equal or proper as I sit here and sip my coffee because this was what people did back then just to try and be seen as more. Sit in a café and dink coffee and many would happily pay twenty dollars for no more than four drinks all because we were convinced it was something people had to have and something we needed. I guess that was one of the things people wrongfully believed in. We'd not want to risk being seen without a cup of coffee due to fear of how others would see us; we didn't want to be seen as lacking so we convinced ourselves that it was a necessity.

We went on believing in things and having little to no faith in each other, turning our backs on people while allowing ourselves to be taken advantage of all for "luxuries," the most easily spread happened to be coffee. Granted a false sense of comfort in many wrongly established luxuries.

It's funny how things work out I suppose. Now our luxuries are simple. What we need we know we can get and what we want does not overshadow what is essential. It is basic living and survival. Obviously perfection will never be possible but a utopian society is not and should never be the goal, simplicity is.

Maybe that's what he meant when he was talking about chance and logical consequences. For us now we take chances on each other, and in the past we made it more important to take chances on the things that would make us better than one another. There in lay the biggest problem, our over bearing and insatiable appetite to prove that there is such a thing as Better and Best within a society. We manifested power in the form of tangibles: money, class and religions. We allowed ourselves to get so involved with making each other look bad that in the end, our selfishness and greed consumed our humanity. It wasn't until we lost it that we recognized how badly we needed it to survive.

"Maybe for him playing with the kids and sneaking a kiss or two to the baker, is how he nourishes his humanity. Maybe for him this small act and continuing to believe in something that has a high chance of not happening, is his way of bringing balance to life."

Then again, I could be wrong.

"Maybe that is the reward of risk, the unknown possibility of it all and being able to accept all that comes with the unknown. While the beauty of a chance is learning to be greater than what the past has dictated us to be. After all, it has been said that realizing how little one knows is the beginning of learning what really matters."

Truth

I sat twirling the empty cup in my hand. Spinning it in a way that resembled how a cowboy would spin a gun before putting it into its holster. It was peaceful here in his coffee shop, well it was a bit hectic really but for me it brought solace. There was a lot going on around me but after spending such a tiring night alone in an abandoned apartment, it was soothing to have other people around me.

The woman with the book seemed remarkably unbothered by all that was going on around her. The espresso machine was buzzing constantly, milk was being steamed and the odd man in the mismatched suit was talking to himself loud enough for anyone else who came in to hear. All of this was going on and it didn't bother me because I didn't have to think about anything.

At the most I wondered what book the lady was reading and what the man was writing down in his journal as he talked to himself. Other than that, I had no thoughts, none what so ever. I just sat there enjoying the scenery through the window and playing my part in what was going on inside.

The sun had gained its peak position in the sky and the streets and shops around them were now busy with traffic. There were families trying to keep together in the crowds, children tugging on the arms of their parents towards toys or treats in the windows that caught their attention. Shopkeepers were either trying to gain the attention of passers by or attending to those who decided to go into their shops.

Across the street and back towards the way I came, the art place I passed by still looked closed. No sign of the owner and no sign of anyone showing interest in what might be inside.

I wonder if the bookstore next door is as unlucky with customers as the art shop. Why isn't the owner of that art there to sell it? The street is plenty busy; there are plenty of opportunities to sell something.

I was so focused on what was going on outside that I didn't notice the cafe owner walk up and stand right next to my chair. He was quiet for a moment and just stared in the same direction I did before he leaned over and whispered, "All finished with that or did you want to hold onto it for a bit longer?"

"No you can take it, I think I am done with it now. Thank you umm, I'm sorry I never caught your name."

"You can call me Ernie."

"How long were you standing there?"

"Not long, I didn't want to interrupt you but you have been playing with my mug for a while and I am afraid you might drop it and break it. I know it isn't pretty but I don't have too many of them to spare."

"Oh, I'm sorry. Its kind of something I do when I am thinking, twitch my fingers. If there happens to be an object in my hand then I toss it around without noticing really."

"I have some broken ones I don't use if you want a substitute for this one."

"No thank you, I think I will be alright now."

"So, what is it that has your attention with the market?"

"All of it really but Ernie, how come the art place over there isn't open?"

"You would have to ask the owner for that."

"Where is he?"

"You mean, where is she? She is sitting right over there, reading a book The Definition of Proper Art."

"Oh okay, what is her name?"

"That's Sasha. She looks like you should be afraid of her but it's a front she puts on. She just, doesn't like people wasting her time."

"Okay then. Thanks Ernie."

"You're welcome, umm, what was your name again?"

"Ernie! I have so much to tell you, so many great things. And good news for you too I must say." The loud woman burst through the door in a way that startled everyone and had I not had coffee to help wake me up, she would have done so with her entrance.

"Sorry about her, she can be pretty loud and oblivious. That's…"

"Martha I assume?"

"Yea, that's Martha. You and I will talk a little later. Or maybe a lot later, this may take a while."

"No problem. I think I can find something to do until then."

I walked over to the woman sitting near the pastries. "Excuse me, Miss Sasha? Do you mind if I ask you a question?"

"That depends on the question."

"I was just wondering if, your art shop is down the street and people are out and about buying things, why aren't you out there trying to get their attention?"

She looked up at me and then over my shoulder at the market. She closed her book gently and placed it between us on the table.

"Take a seat and I will tell you why. You see the thing with art is, it requires a certain type of eye to notice it and understand its worth and beauty. The people outside don't have this kind of eye."

"But don't you think that if they saw you out there with your art, they would stop and want to know what you have?"

"I have tried that, I have tried displaying the different art I have out front with me but nobody has stopped to purchase it in a long time."

"That is unfortunate, I'm sorry to hear that. When I passed by it this morning, it seemed like there were some amazing things inside."

"You liked what you saw?"

"Yes, I don't remember the last time I saw a piece of art like that up close."

"Well what did you see? What did you think?"

"The only things I could make out really are the glass figurine and dish set in the window. The figurine looked to me like it was people dancing."

"That is what I saw too. You know, that piece happened completely by accident. I was trying to make an extended and abstract piece of glass to hang from my ceiling. I thought that if that one went well, I could try to make wind chimes, something people would be able to enjoy and not need to find a place for them."

"Did you end up making any wind chimes?"

"No, I don't even think I tried."

"How come?"

"I just got wrapped up in the dancers. I tried time and time again to recreate what I had done but it never happened. The reason they are the colors they are is because when they melted all the other colors blended together, that isn't suppose to happen. There used to be purple and greens and blues and reds and a bit of white as well. Now it is just the two colors. I don't even know where the gold came from."

"They are beautiful though. Even an accidental success such as that one has the possibility to happen again."

"Yes, but it is a very small opportunity."

"True but don't all big moments start off as small opportunities? It just takes a lot of time and practice to create small moments on a bigger scale. Isn't that part of what art is?"

"What do you mean?"

"I mean, isn't art the collected gathering of small moments that help create a bigger one?"

"In a way I guess that makes sense. But recreating something like the dancers seems pretty much impossible."

"Maybe it seems impossible because you are focusing on the wrong aspect of the art. Instead of focusing on trying to recreate the same sculpture, focus your thoughts and energy on how creating something new makes you feel. It is the process and imperfections that make art so unique and mesmerizing, not the outcome of what was done."

"I guess I don't really know when that last time was that I just, felt what I was doing with my work."

"What about the plates and cups? The ones that look like they represent the four elements?"

"Oh yes, those were on purpose. After trying to recreate the dancers I went back to see what shapes and designs I could make and then cups and plates came the easiest. I have always had an appreciation for nature. It was my inspiration for much of my life and so putting it into glass just made sense. Even though it really bothers me that I only have that one set of dancers, the cups and plates came to me freely. With the dancers, could you imagine having different ones in different colors and different positions? It would symbolize a coming together of all kinds of people. Different shapes and sizes, colors, backgrounds. Different amounts of time spent on each one. Some would be separated form their partners and others would be connected just by the slightest touch. And made out of glass, the symbolism, the sheer delicacy of the entire outcome. Do you think people would connect to it? Do you think they would be able to see themselves in the art?"

"I don't think everyone would but a few for sure. I would like to think I would be one of the few."

"You know, I wouldn't even care if people wanted to buy the dancers. I would just be happy to have something amazing that people could come in and just marvel at."

"Forgive me if I am wrong but, isn't the point of art to just be seen and observed? I understand the desire to make sure something will inspire and strike awe into all who happen upon it. I just don't think that should be the main motivation behind art. Any art really."

"I suppose I can see your point."

"For example, the wind chime idea you had. That was simple enough that people who bought one would have enjoyed them and people who didn't could have enjoyed just hearing the sound it made and seeing a simple design change in the light. To you that may not be a marvelous idea but to a particular family or a person who lives on their own, it could make all the difference on a cold day."

"Haven't you ever wondered if something you did or thought was good enough?"

"Yes, more times then I can really remember but I think that the only reason that happens is to show us how unaware we are of our own potential. It is scary to know we could possibly fail but equally scary to know that we can just as well succeed."

"Do you think it is ever too late to try? Is it ever too late to accomplish an idea?"

"I think that it is only too late if someone believes it is. It can really go either way; it's really just a matter of perspective. It's always a good idea to look at something with hope though. Even if it seems like it is pointless to do so, a little hope can go a long way."

The last sentence caught her off guard because she gave me a look that suggested I struck a nerve. "All the best things begin with hope."

"Yes, yes they do. Is that something you believe?"

"I used to a long time ago. I guess I just let myself forget it."

"The good thing about forgetting is knowing you have something to look forward to once you remember."

"You look very young how is it you know so much?"

"I just reflect on what it is I see in the world and in others really. I basically speak my mind but not a lot of people have appreciated it."

"No, most people wouldn't. A lot of people, in my experience, say they would prefer the truth but don't really like it once they hear it. It's more like they want to hear what they think, not what is really true."

"I know what you mean. I've lost a lot of people in my life because of that very misunderstanding."

"The truly good people will want to keep you around and invite you further into their lives, so don't you worry about those who push you away."

"Thank you Sasha. I have to admit, I am glad we crossed paths."

"May I ask you something, why is it you liked the dancers so much?"

"It seemed romantic. A moment of romance suspended in time in the arch of the female partner and held onto by the hands of the male. Because for the rest of time they have to believe in one another, they have to let the other one know that they will always be there. I didn't know it at the time but it is an example of what life is all about. Staying true and having faith in each other, plus it's nice to see a bit of romanticism around despite all that has happened."

"You have been talking to Ernie haven't you?"

"A little bit before anyone got here this morning. How did you know?"

"He has said similar things to me before but for some reason hearing you say it makes a difference."

"How is that?"

"Because everything you just said, you said without fear, hesitation or regret, it came from your soul. As if you believe it and have always believed it. I used to feel the same way about my art so I guess I see a bit of who I used to be in you. It seems to me the time has come to once again start living in the moment."

"Well I am glad I could help. I was worried I would waste your time asking you about your shop."

"No, not at all. It was something that I think had to happen."

I am starting to think it was no coincidence me coming into Ernie's café, or for me to have stayed in that apartment all night.

"Good luck to you Sasha. Hopefully I will see a wind chime in front of your shop the next time I come around."

"Not just that but a few more dancers too."

It made me feel good to know that I had helped Sasha regain her sense of vision. It had not at all been my intention but I think that made it even better. Sasha was sitting in her chair, as if searching her mind for more lost art ideas. I sat there too, turned sideways in the chair thinking of the thin line separating strength and weakness.

I guess we all have a certain amount of potential within us. We all have a strength that could easily become a weakness if we allow the tiniest of circumstances to cloud our vision. Yet, thriving beneath this shared vulnerability is honesty. Individual inner truths that are meant to be expressed because in our most vulnerable of times, we find guidance and compassion and share a bigger portion of who we are with each other. Maybe we are meant to find and appreciate our individual weaknesses so that we can share them with one another and create an ever-lasting strength.

As I walked back to my original table, Sasha picked up her book, smiled and waved good-bye to me. She gave a hurried wave to Ernie as she walked out of the door and Ernie waved back, which distracted Martha for a moment but then she turned right back to pick up where she left off. Maybe it was where she left off; her hands were going all over the place as she talked, I couldn't imagine what was going on in the conversation between she and him.

Poor Ernie, I don't think I have heard him really get a word in since she came in here.

As I sat down I saw that the shadow of the tree outside the window had shifted a good distance from where it was before. I leaned over to the skittish man who, in Martha's grand entrance, had dropped the other half of his pastry on the floor. He didn't seem to notice until I interrupted his writing, "Excuse me, what time would you guess it is?"

"Oh, I don't need to guess, I have a watch. Its quarter after two."

"Okay. You know, you dropped your pastry."

"I did? Hmm, I did. Thank you."

"No problem. Thank you for the time."

"Of course."

Then I noticed something about the notebook he had with him. All the pages were filled, from front to back, full of notes and doodles. It didn't look very organized, there were some things written vertically and others written from side to side, arrows pointing to certain sentences and then others crossed out entirely.

"Umm, if you don't mind me asking, what is that you have there?"

"Oh this, its just something I have been working on here and there. In fact, every so often I come in here just to add more things to it. Ernie sets a good atmosphere here. It's very easy for me to get a lot done. Just my espresso and my notebook and then I lose track of time."

"Is it all one thing that you write about in it?"

"Oh, it's not just things I write, it's things I hear or see or think about. Sometimes I don't feel like writing, so I draw, and other times I don't feel like doing either one so I just look at the pages until something new is presented to me."

"So then, it's about life?"

"I guess so, yes. It is more or less a collection of lives and different things they mean. It's quite a lot to explain but if I had to some it up I would say it started really with a theory. A theory of conspiracy; as we, not just you and I but all people, in and throughout history, have grown to conspire to only show the best parts of who we are and sometimes we attempt to alter history to do so."

"So its about history then?"

"No, no, not entirely. See I own the bookstore next door. Did you see the name?"

"No, I passed by it but I didn't even think to look for a name. I was just wondering why it was closed. I wanted to see if I could find a book I found in an apartment in there. To see if it was something well known."

"Oh okay, well, the name is Lost Books. I have a whole bunch of everything in there. What is the book you found?"

"Oh, it's a black book. No name on the cover and no title. Not any kind of clue as to what might be in it. I just don't want to open it and be disappointed, you know?"

"No, I don't know. I have never opened a book and been disappointed. Each one is unique and valuable in its own right."

"Wait, if you own the bookstore, why aren't you there now? Why isn't it open?"

"I closed it today. For me the first market of the month is always slow. So I am using the opportunity to get some things written down that have been on my mind for a while now. As far as what I am writing today, because I know you are going to ask, I am just trying to put all ideas and concepts in one location where people can get to them and understand the difference between past and present."

"So you have been trying to gather as much information as possible in order to, change back the changes that have been made to our history?"

"Yes, except you can't change back what has already been done; you can only hope to influence a better outcome for what may happen in the future. What we read of history and what we are told is, for the most part, something we accept based on our idea of faith."

"Ernie and I were just talking about this. We only touched on the topic a little but he told me that faith is basically not being able to see something but knowing it is there."

"Yes, imagine walking through a room blindfolded. You have no choice but to stick out your arms and feel your way around, hoping you don't run into something and hurt yourself or break something valuable. Now with our history, whether it be personal or world wide, we are told exactly where things are in the room so that we can easily navigate our path. What if, we were to take off the blindfold? What if when we did so, we found out that we weren't just standing in a room blindfolded, we were standing in a huge house and it was pitch black inside? We would be under the impression that something was wrong."

"You mean like someone betrayed us?"

"Yes and no. I mean we betrayed ourselves. Because we stood somewhere with no idea where we were or what had happened before we got there and neglected to ask ourselves why we were there or where we should be going. We just felt our way around a small portion of a greater area. Yes, faith is accepting the idea of not being able to see certain things and that is important for a person to have; but blind faith grants no clarity to it's holder."

"So all of what you have on every page are facts to support this theory?"

"No what I have are experiences, both mine and those I have seen and collected from observing others. Just like a book, each and every one of us has our own history; we all have our own story to tell. I don't want to make history, I want to record it for someone or many later on to see and understand. To be able to relate to it in ways that were often over looked in the history books of before. You see there is no way to learn what mistakes not to make and what lessons to pass on if only half of all of them are recorded. Please excuse me, I think I am going to have to write this little conversation of ours down."

I hadn't even gotten to say okay before he frantically flipped to a new page. He started to feel around for his pastry and then he moved his foot and I could see he felt it crunch under the tip of his shoe. He picked it up and pinched a piece of lint off of it, took a small bite out of it, and then he twirled his pen in his hand between his figures. A few crumbs fell on his book; he picked it up and shook them loose.

Odd man, not the kind of conversation I would have expected from him really.

I could understand what he was saying though. It all made sense even though I was sure his notebook was just a cluster of nonsense. The gist of what he said was the truth, which was, we had allowed ourselves to get used to an idea. We allowed ourselves to settle into a way of living because it was comfortable not because it was right. We let who we really were dwindle away bit by bit because we took it upon ourselves to make the choice for others the kinds of lives they should be living.

Thinking back on it now, the stories I have heard and certain parts of old things I have read, that is how it was. It's sad really, to know that so many people were denied the ability to be happy. All because certain groups and people were afraid to change small parts of whom they were for the betterment of others. It's just another example of uncompromising common courtesy, the very beginning of the loss of our humanity.

I was born into a belief system; a kind of religion that, I have been told was one of the top religions in the world, but I have heard the opposite from others. I was raised within certain traditions and expected to be a certain way because that is how others before me had behaved. I did, I prayed the way I was told I should pray, I went to the ceremonies I was told to go to, I even tried to be friends with only those that were raised to believe in the same way I was. I did all of this and more without question until I reached the age of nineteen. Then I began to wonder, I began to drift away from my religious expectation. I didn't do so in the prospect of negating everything I was told or taught but more so because I wanted to gain different experiences and expand upon the beauty of lessons I had been taught. To put into practice what it is I was told I had to do but saw no one else, who was raised in the same expectations, doing.

I was told it should not matter of the beliefs of others because each and every one of us has something bigger than who we are that we believe in. That to love one another no matter what was the very purpose that we had all been put into this world. That learning to love oneself is only the beginning of a greater purpose of which we are all connected to. When the time came, I asked some of my teachers why things were they way they were and had been, even though so many people had been taught and endowed with this base of existing, they said: "Not everyone could be like us. We are special and gifted in ways that others are not fortunate enough to be, so we must show them our ways. That way they too can be as blessed as us."

That statement still to this day makes no sense to me. So many people are taught that everyone is equal yet, are later expected to adhere to jaded understandings that only those who embraced in what or who is said to be good are truly good. That everyone who is not part of that group has to marvel at someone else's greatness. That only one opinion matters, all others are unimportant or insignificant. All this created was hypocritical hysteria. It's no wonder he wants to put more perspective on what will one day be history.

My choice to embark on a more spiritual journey didn't sit well with a lot of people, especially those who had performed many of my "rights of passage" ceremonies, but I knew it would be better. It was and had always been my nature to be curious and question things and it had always escorted me to betterment and personal growth. Even though most often my questions were met with trying and difficult obstacles, it was always worth it in the end. To stand victorious in a shadow that once overpowered my presence.

Through that journey I learned many things. Most of the time, lessons and certain ideas repeated themselves. It was fascinating to me how even though a lot of these religions and beliefs had been based in different parts of the world, all of them had one thing in common, the soul purpose of bringing people together. It was all about unity through, love, patience, passion, determination, character, wisdom and much more. I was able to talk to a few people from different belief backgrounds and all of them expressed the desire to achieve the most overlooked attributes of life. Not all of them had the same way of living but all of them wanted just one thing, to live happily. Not sheltered from pain and fear or burdened by false expectations, just to be and help others to be.

What we believe is of small significance; the important things are why we believe and how we act on what we believe in. It is and has never been enough to be told that there is or is not someone there. Nor has it been enough to be told that we should see something in a way that others before us have; before we knew there was something to be seen.

It is impossible to believe in anything, to acknowledge there is something more that we cannot see if a person refuses to open up their heart and mind. All that can do is force people to fit into a mold, one that is wrongly depicted as personifying perfection. Then it becomes not about belief but entitlement. Starting to share the responsibility of knowing that none of us have to be perfect can change everything.

There is no way for any of us to know the truth of how we began but we should work together to ensure that the world continues, that life continues.

"Alright, I'm back. That woman can talk all day and in fact, she has once. I barely got anything done but sometimes you have to just let people say what they want to say because to them it's important. So, what did I miss? I saw you talking to Joseph and Sasha before she left, how was that?"

"It wasn't too bad, not really what I expected. Sasha and I talked about art and what it means and she told me the different things she wanted to do but stopped pursuing."

"Sounds like a good talk, why did she leave?"

"Oh, I think I helped her see why it is important not to give up on something just because you grow weary of uncertainty. How it is important to push on through what seems impossible because all new things seem impossible at first."

"Really? That is what you said?"

"Well, something along those lines. I don't really remember because it was in the moment."

"You saying what you said got her to go and open up her shop again?"

"I don't know if she is opening it up today but I think she is getting started on a few ideas she had for her glass works. Starting from a few of the basics so she can build up to who she wants to be."

"I see. I have been trying to get her to go back for a while now and then you come in here and change everything; I have been saying the exact same thing to her. I don't get it. What about Joseph? You get him to go and sell his books or something?"

"No, he and I just talked. Rather he talked and I just sat there and listened. Tried not to intrude on his train of thought because it seemed like he knew where he was going."

"Yea, that is true. I am hesitant to stop him a lot of the time. When he and I first talked I was surprised too. I thought he would be much more frantic and scattered. I mean he was but, I think that is his way of warming up to people."

"Yea, I could see that. It was good though. How long has he been working on that book?"

"I don't know what color is it?"

"I'm not sure, I think its green. I didn't get a good look at it really. He flipped it open too fast."

"Well if it's a green one, it's a new book. Last week he had a grey one."

"You mean he did all of that in a week? It's more than half way finished."

"I know he works fast. I think his mind is as vivid and obscure as his outfits, but it suits him. He is a good man."

"Yea he is, odd but good. Have you heard his history conspiracy theory?"

"Oh yes, that is a good one. It's not as far fetched as some of the conspiracy theories I have heard in my day either. I could actually follow along with it. His collection of books at the store is astounding."

"I could imagine so."

"No, I don't mean just printed books I mean journals and scraps of paper he finds laying around on the streets. He makes scrapbooks out of those. He lives to gather things, that way he can leave as much information behind as possible for other people to learn from."

"Really? Journals too? So he just asks people if he can have them to keep at the store or what?"

"Sometimes, but a lot of people around here know him so if they find something they think is interesting or they have a journal they think would help his collection, they give it to him."

"Interesting. You know, I found a book at the place I was staying at. I haven't opened it up or anything but it has kind of this mysterious air about it."

"You don't say. Where is it you were before you came here?"

"I found an abandoned apartment at the far end of the street. I checked around before I went in and it didn't seem like anyone lived there."

"No, nobody lives there. There was a family there about six months ago but they moved onto the next colony. So are you going to open up this book and see if there is anything good in it?"

"Maybe in a little while. Joseph brought a lot of things to my attention. Things I hadn't really thought about in a while."

"Like what?"

"Just a few things about how religion went from a way to bring people together to a reason to keep everyone divided. The messages meant to inspire love and peace were changed to inflict hate and distrust. Its all a bit depressing."

"Wow, Joseph really did get to you. That's good. Even though everybody knows him, not many people are willing to sit and listen to him or try to make sense of things he says. What brought you to religion, did he say something about it?"

"No, no, its just something that I remember questioning first. The first thing I questioned that gained negative remarks and discouragements."

"Awe, I see. So you were curious about how to apply yourself to your religion, right?"

"No, I was curious as to how I could apply myself to the ideas that span beyond the gates of religions. Curious as to how I could be more than what others had depicted I should be and how I could help others to do the same."

"This kind of correlates to the conversation we were having earlier. About chance, except now you have brought up the variable of curiosity. Which again, is a logical and understandable feeling, especially in terms of something you believe in."

"But what is the saying, 'curiosity killed the cat'?"

"Yes, but something often overlooked is the fact that we are enabled with curiosity from the day we are born. It is simply human nature. To reach out as an infant at a finger because you are uncertain of what it is, so you want to touch it, feel it in your hand and know that it is real. As a baby you have never been told to reach out for something and it is not a concept you really understand it's just an action to you at that point, something you feel you have to do."

"So why is it so bad to be curious and ask questions as you grow up? It is nearly frowned upon, instead people are expected to follow along with what we were told to do just because it is what had always been done."

"Yes, as people grew up, they were slowly and steadily convinced over time not to question the most important things. The things that were said to have the most influence on our lives. Because when questions are asked and people go looking for answers, inevitably things will be lost in the process. A lot of people, people who believed in social standings and the continued manifestation of power in material objects, knew that all of what they had could and would be lost. It wasn't that they had grown attached to these things more like they had become, engrossed by them. They didn't know how to live without them so they made a lot of other people think they too had to have them. Really it just became a disease and spread into an epidemic and then not too long after, people became a plague. Very few would question what would go on and even fewer would listen to those that did."

"You sound like you saw a lot of what happened before."

"I saw it and I was part of it. I did very little to fix things and make sure people, myself included, were happy. I'm very different from who I was before. A lot of people are. I think your talk with Sasha was much needed on her part. She has been back and forth with so many ideas, really good ones too. I was actually getting tired of seeing her sit in here and read book after book, although she and Joseph seemed to become more friendly since she got all her books from him. We all need second chances in life, to understand who we are and why it is we are here."

"How did you change, how did you cope with knowing you played a hand in how things had gotten so bad?"

"One day I woke up and told myself that wasn't who I am anymore. That isn't who I have to be. It is never too late for change and there is always room to take hold of a second chance. It's really just a matter of will and courage. Getting past the prideful part you have in you and becoming something better. You have to believe in yourself, and in doing so learn to believe in others. Even though they can disappoint you, you shouldn't let that be the reason why you don't show them through your actions that you won't disappoint them."

"Take a chance and have faith."

"Exactly. Have faith in yourself and the uncertain. If you do then one way or another everything will work out in the way it should. At least that has been my experience. It's just about lunch time here, do you want to see a menu?"

"In a little bit. I'm thinking about finally opening up this book I have, you know, just to see if it should be put in Joseph's collection or not."

"Alright, well let me know if you find anything good."

"I will, I promise."

I took the book out of my pocket, put my hand on the cover and flipped the corner of it a few times. Feeling the small gusts of air it created flow in between my fingers. I looked out the window and then back at Joseph. He was writing away, like he was on a mission.

"Joseph, what are you writing now?"

"What?"

I must have startled him, either that or he was feeling the effects of the espresso shots he had. *I didn't even see him get up to get more. When did Ernie give them to him?*

"Sorry, I didn't mean to interrupt you."

"It's alright, I tend to drown the rest of the world out when I start to write in my journal."

"Okay, well I'll let you get back to it then."

"Thank you, it shouldn't be too long now."

"What do you mean by that?"

"Huh? Nothing, nothing, I was talking to myself. I didn't mean to say that out loud."

"Okay, you dropped a pen."

"Keep it, I have others. I might get another espresso."

"Okay, why are you telling me?"

"Yes, I will get another."

He is talking to himself out loud again, that is an odd habit to have. Even though, I am sure I have done it at least once or twice.

I turned back towards the window, *Odd, even though so much has gone on earlier in the day and I have been content to see it all through a window, the thought of looking through a window any longer doesn't appeal to me. I think I might go and sit outside for a little bit.*

I sat down under the tree that stood in front of the pile of rubble, with my legs straight out and my feet hanging off of the curb dangling freely only a couple inches from the ground. People still shopped around but it was not as busy as before, outside the art shop I saw Sasha taking measurements. She already had her very own wind chime hanging in front of her door.

The first prototype from when she started them and made the dancers I bet. It looks good. People are already starting to take notice.

I felt the sun hitting my skin and warming my clothes. I took off my jacket and folded it in my lap. I tried twirling the pen in my fingers just as Joseph had, it wasn't as easy as it looked but it was fun to do anyway. On my right sat the book, unopened, unknown, and I was no longer bothered by it. I flipped the edges of the pages again from the top of the book to the bottom, it's black cover quickly turning from black to white and then black again.

A breeze came up and above me the leaves in the tree began to shake and shimmy just as they had when I was a kid down in my memorable safe haven. It felt good; it felt like this is where I was supposed to be.

We had grown so used to looking at the world through a window as a society. For an entire night that is all I did, trying to make sense of so many things. Doing it all on my own and even though it worked for a while I soon realized I needed something more. The window provided me with a high vantage point, yes, and I could see down the street and on top of roofs and even into other buildings but eventually I was blocked by my own reflection. When I wanted to see more I couldn't because I was getting in my own way. I guess what it comes down to is, knowing that a window will only allow you to see so much. Eventually you and your will, or lack thereof, begin to reflect in it. It loses its ability and becomes more and more restricted the longer you stare.

Perhaps that is what made the world so crazy before. Thinking each and every one of us had to figure everything out on our own. Getting too wrapped up in how important we wanted to be that we neglected the importance of all the people who could have an impact in our lives.

There is no need to be concerned with people calling me a lunatic because what some may see as crazy I now classify as accepting. I am willing to accept a possibility that triumphs a previous possibility I didn't think was possible. Being willing to learn that what I thought was impossible is possible for someone else and that the same goes for me in his or her eyes, allowing for more common ground to be found and shared between us. Why is that crazy?

Inside the cafe I could see the lunch menus being passed around. No one picked it up right away but it didn't seem to bother Ernie. He was really patient and I couldn't imagine him being the opposite before any of us knew him. I wasn't feeling very hungry just yet besides; I promised Ernie I would let him know if there was anything good in the book. I picked it up and put it on my lap as I flicked the pen with my ring and middle finger.

I took a deep breath and slowly opened the book to the first page, then quickly turned to the next page and then the next one, and then opened the book all the way to the middle.

"…Of course."

I couldn't help but smile and chuckle a bit at what I saw inside. It was empty. "This whole time..." I was at a loss; I felt a combination of both amazement and welcome.

I honestly did not see this coming. I don't think Ernie is going to believe it either, or perhaps he will. In any case I guess this won't be getting added to Joseph's collection...

"Then again, maybe it will…"

I looked at the pen in my hand and down at the first blank page as it sat in the book, vacant yet intriguing. I imagined the book was equally surprised with me for opening it now, after having neglected it for so long. It seemed to have held onto to its own portion of the air from the apartment, letting bits of it go slowly with seemingly small breaths of anticipation as it waited to see what I would do next. That shared nervous moment of appreciation between us allowed for an understanding to be reached, we both knew why we had crossed paths as we were brought back to where we first met.

I smiled and uncapped the pen because I knew what I was going to do. I smiled out of the corner of my mouth, took in a big breath and started writing:

For as long as I can remember I had been questioning the world around me, questioning its meaning and inquiring for it to include me so that I would no longer feel disconnected...

CPSIA information can be obtained
at www.ICGtesting.com
Printed in the USA
FSOW01n0544120315
5629FS